"Through the lens of an everyday middle school girl with an aptitude for both humanities and science, readers will become rapt by Charley's enchanting world. Her infectious love for STEM will inspire all inquiring minds."

—Michaela A. James, 14

"Action, adventure, suspense, and, dare I say, some romance are what await you in *Saving Time*. Payes captures the true teenage spirit of heroism, friendship, and passion for knowledge, while paving the way for new adventures in STEM and teaching us quantum physics in the process."

—Stephen Hodges, author of *The Magic Poof*

"I recommend this book to my friends because it's intriguing, and time seems to go by quickly when reading. I learned that Leonardo, Michelangelo, and Raphael were not just Ninja Turtles, lol."

—Ricardo A. Carrillo, 12

"My son (Ricardo) and I read the book together, which was a great experience. We did research as we read, and it ended up being a great learning opportunity for both of us. I appreciated that there were life lessons learned that all readers could relate to. I even found myself laughing out loud to some of Charley's comments. Overall, it was a great read."

—Vanessa Carrillo,
Director of Columbia University Girls in STEM program

"*Saving Time* really captures the full essence of adventure, friendship, and a love of history, all in one. Each page will have you on the edge of your seat, wanting to know how this incredible story ends!"

—Sydney Johnson, Edge of Yesterday intern, student at George Mason University

"It's a wonderful thing when an author can weave a story where history meets fiction. Charley Morton represents the Renaissance girl that all young women have the potential to be, and for this reason, *Saving Time* is an educator's dream. Charley restores my faith in questioning the world and being fearless in the face of adversity. Another great read by Robin Stevens Payes."

—Tosin Adetoro, owner of Get Into STEM, LLC, and STEAM educator

The Edge of Yesterday series
A Multimedia Teen Time Travel Adventure
www.edgeofyesterday.com
Transforming STEAM learning through story

Learning never exhausts the mind.
~Leonardo da Vinci

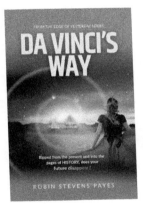

LIFE IN THE TIME OF A NOVEL CORONAVIRUS: A TIME CAPSULE

2020 Saving Time

Dear historians from the future,

Whenever you may find this, we are encrypting this time capsule in the summer of Earth Year 2020. We hope that whoever, wherever, and whenever you are, you find yourself whole, hearty, and healthy.

We are living through weird times. It's not that periods of existential threat, fear, and uncertainty have never popped up before in human history—the Inquisition; the bubonic plague, cholera, and the 1918 Spanish flu pandemic; and the American Civil War, World Wars I and II, and the Holocaust all come to mind.

But never before has humanity across the globe been *so instantly interconnected* to the reality of takedown by an invisible enemy that threatens the health, institutions, economy, livelihood, and well-being of our entire planet all at once.

Never before in recorded history have we faced such global dangers like climate change and COVID-19 that could take down humanity in ways that all the wars before could not. But it is our internal response to threat that has the most potential for lasting harm. Mostly, it upsets the *illusion* that we have ever been in control of any of it.

We're living through *tempus disruptus*: a rupture in time.

I am the author of a time travel, science fiction adventure series of books for teens. My young American time traveler and *STEAMinista* (if you're among the uninitiated, that's a girl who wants to learn and do *everything* under the sun), Charley Morton, finds herself unexpectedly transported to plague-ridden destinations over centuries. It's part of what's inspired her to pursue a career in forensic anthropology—unraveling the story of humankind through the history of disease.

Exposure to the historical evidence of diseases, and the social and cultural disruptions as she encounters them in real time, from the past in which they occur, are what guide her Indiana Jones–like approach to solving disease mysteries across time.

Because she comes from a time of more advanced medical understanding, technology, and treatment, when vaccines and herd immunities have vanquished viral and bacterial contagions like smallpox and polio, Charley is immune from the scourge of such past outbreaks.

In doing research for *Edge of Yesterday*, I was fascinated to learn that the Black Death was not spread by rats, as common wisdom had it, but by Asian gerbils hitchhiking on shipments along then-prosperous sea trading routes or along the Silk Road. I've dug into the facts about the mass warehousing of plague victims' corpses above Paris cemeteries when they were too numerous to be buried—and the gravediggers themselves falling victim to the disease—in cemeteries like Les Innocents, which was right next to Paris's largest marketplace.

In 2020 that same academic curiosity came crashing into reality, wearing the costume of COVID-19, with its own theories of spread, confusion about causes, and the ensuing catastrophe—rising death tolls, a crash of health systems, chaos, and panic in the face of uncertainty. In the U.S., the powers that be have led a less than robust response.

As we focus on existing in our own time, in our own homes, without the "normal" routines and busyness that give us the illusion of control, we're left to our imaginations, to follow an untrodden path through this inevitable rupture toward recovery. Ultimately, we see that the only control we have is how we respond to whatever black swan events life throws our way.

Out of chaos can come creativity, innovation, collaboration, unity, and love . . . if we so choose. That is my hope for humanity at this time.

Only history will know the outcome. So please, future historians, if you can get word back across time, let us know how we all turn out!

Your Partner in Time Travel (PITT),
Robin Stevens Payes
author and creator, The Edge of Yesterday series
www.edgeofyesterday.com

Saving Time

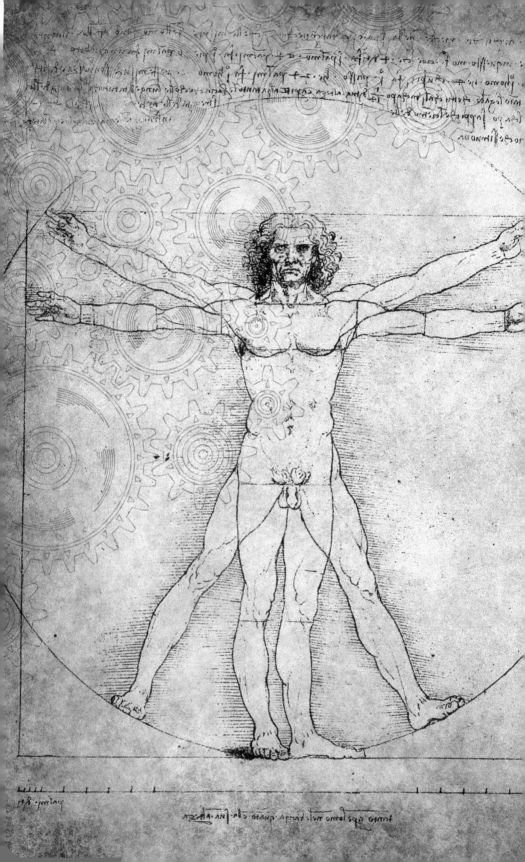

Saving Time

Edge of Yesterday
Book III

by Robin Stevens Payes

Printed in the United States of America

Cover design by Melissa Brandstatter
Interior design by Lisa Vega
Interior composition by Megan Katsanevakis

Images courtesy of Creative Commons/Wikimedia and Robin Stevens Payes

Library of Congress Control Number: 2020910880
ISBN: 978-1-951568-06-1

SMALL
BATCH
BOOKS

493 SOUTH PLEASANT STREET
AMHERST, MASSACHUSETTS 01002
413.230.3943
SMALLBATCHBOOKS.COM

For all those who ask, who dream, and dare,
walking the edge together.

Special thanks to my EOY Media co-creators: Lindsay, Claire,
Ileana, Ashley, Hannah, Grace, Jared, Dashajnae, and Kiara.
Get inspired by their work at edgeofyesterday.com.

Fire destroys all sophistry, that is deceit; and maintains truth alone, that is gold.

—Leonardo da Vinci

Contents

THE EDGE OF YESTERDAY:
COMING BACK TO THE CODA

(*Coda*: a musical term that is Italian for the ending of a song or a dance—but also, like, The Last Word.)

I'm dreaming, I know it. I have built a time machine spurred on by a drawing, a vision, and a school project. Somehow, it worked.

Inside my dream, I wake up in the deep past. Except it is now my present: five hundred years until the present. I have no idea what my future holds, or if I even have one!

I revisit the facts: school science fair, found Leonardo da Vinci's plans for a time machine, but he didn't have technology or science to build it . . . but twenty-first century, different story. Blah, blah, blah. And since I'm determined to be a modern-day Leonardo, I'm the girl who's gonna prove time travel's not only possible, but I have made it happen! So I am sojourning (isn't that a good word? It means to reside somewhere temporarily. God, I pray that this is only temporary!) in a faraway past—1492, to be precise, in Florence, Italy, when it isn't even really Italy (and has somehow not caught on to the delectable tastiness of spaghetti and pizza yet . . . I mean, who knew?!). I have actually met Leonardo da Vinci face-to-face, and I don't mean an impersonator or, like, Leonardo DiCaprio playing the Renaissance genius.

I AM NOT KIDDING.

And there's a whole lot of drama going on here! Like Leonardo is totally gonzo over my tablet that is showing him the future that he now is determined to invent. Including painting the *Mona Lisa* ('cause history says he won't actually start to paint it for another ten years). So we're talking time paradox here, and it's my fault.

And that's just the start! There's this preacher, Savonarola, who is totally anti-technology. In fact, he's convinced people they need to burn all the books, paintings, furs, jewels, and wigs, for God's sake, so people are gathering every day in the piazza of Florence to hear him speak, then heaping all their priceless possessions (imagine—we are talking about Michelangelo's sketches for his sculptures, Botticelli's paintings, and lots of jewels, furs, gold, and stuff!) onto a giant pyramid, thirty feet high, to be burned! A bonfire of the vanities, it's called. And, as Kairos so delicately pointed out earlier (ahem!), if this Savonarola dude were somehow to get wind of my tablet and phone (thank goodness I figured out how to make a portable battery to keep my devices charged!), he would no doubt turn me in for foretelling the future. A future, I might add, he would disavow as heretical if he were ever to live to see it. And have me burned at the stake. So, if his followers, the Weepers, catch me, I'm gonna be toast. Literally!

Meanwhile, back at home in my own time, my mom may be dying (how I have gleaned that fact from here is a whole 'nother story!); my former best friend, Beth, a time travel skeptic, is busy bad-mouthing me to her new crush, Lex; my science fair partner, Billy, and I are mysteriously able to communicate back and forth through an app he invented called TeenWords; and this whole thing seems to have been hacked into behind the scenes by this odd dude named Kairos, who appears to be neither here, nor there, but everywhere, and in both times at once!

Got that? Okay, me neither.

The good news—Leonardo is totally on board with my mission to reengineer time to help me get back home to the present. Er, the future. Or whatever. I have some new friends here—Elisabetta (or Bethy II), who is my age, and little Carolina, who's like this eight-year-old genius—who are a little behind the times (for our time, that is), but otherwise totally cool.

In spite of all the cool stuff that time travel has wrought, this Renaissance Florence is not a safe place. Book burnings, gypsy caravans that kidnap unsuspecting time travelers, bandits, Lorenzo de' Medici and his merry henchmen (NOT!), the filthy Arno River, no indoor plumbing . . .

I have no idea whether I will ever make it back in time to win the science fair, but we are not yet out of time!

Adventure of a lifetime? We have barely scratched the surface here. Now I know firsthand that time does not run in a straight line. And it is hardly predictable.

Do my findings contradict the laws of the universe? It will take smarter minds than mine to figure that one out.

Or maybe it's my destiny to be the one to prove the theory of parallel universes. That would be cool. If I have a future, that is.

Just in case, I am collecting evidence as I go.

For now, I am praying that my messages reach Billy in whatever future is happening centuries from now—hopefully one where I exist. And, mostly, I pray for Mamma to be okay. And for me not to have messed up history.

Because, frankly, it's all turning into one big, confusing, terrifying mess.

I.
WHICH WITCH?

A sharp waft of ammonia mixed with awful perfume tickles my nose, followed by a burst of air. *"Achoo!"* I open my eyes—someone's waving this awful odor under my nose.

Did I lose it? When I come to, I hear many voices. I blink a few times—can't tell what I'm looking at. A domed ceiling painted with cherubim and shepherds and shepherdesses in a pale blue, cloudless sky. So I guess this would be heaven?

If so, heaven's far from sterile. Elisabetta, a.k.a. Bethy II, is fanning me with a feather duster; I don't dare think about the dust mites and allergens she must be stirring up.

"This foul-smelling alchemy could wake the dead," Bethy is saying. At least that's what I imagine she's saying, given the stench. I am vaguely aware of being stretched out on the hard couch. Bethy's on a chair next to me and I need to figure out where I am, but my head starts spinning when I try to lift it.

"Oy! When did I pass out?"

"Oy? Che dice?" It's the woman from the guardhouse who let us in earlier.

"E mia madre?" I ask, hoping Bethy will know something. Last I remember, Mamma had passed out at the Pitti Palace in another time

and Kairos was there, but I'm hoping that was all a figment of my imagination.

"*Sua madre! Viola, l'hai sentito?*" squawks a woman's loud voice. I can't make out the words.

Where am I? I look around, dazed, and squint to bring the scene into focus, but it's all fuzzy. It begins to register that I am still in olden-days Florence, that Mamma is in future Florence, and all is not well in the world.

Why, though?

I turn to figure out the voice behind me—one that would appear to belong to Signora Vincenzo, Elisabetta's mom. It doesn't take twenty-twenty vision for me to see her point a finger at her temple and make a circular motion in what must be the universal sign language for crazy.

When did la Vincenza arrive?

Confusion notwithstanding, I push myself up on my elbows, biting back tears. "I want *mia madre!*"

But before I can gather my thoughts, the world begins spinning around me again, and Bethy II reaches out a hand to grab me before I collapse.

"*Ecco, Carlotta!*" Seems Bethy has somehow found Translator and is fitting it over my ears. "*Non puoi capire senza questi.*"

"Huh?" Though Translator appears to be working just fine, my ears aren't tuned in. My senses, it would seem, haven't quite connected with my brain. It's like someone's hacked into my head and completely rewired it.

As she resumes her fanning, Bethy passes the feathers too close, and they tickle my face. "*Achoo!*"

"*Alla salute!*" says Signora Vincenzo. "*Non è principessa come Cleopatra che ha bisogno del vostro ventaglio!*"

Bethy, looking confused, suspends her duster midair. "Cleopatra?"

I catch enough of this to seize on the name of the Egyptian princess, and my mind flashes an image of Cleopatra reclining on a barge floating on the Nile River, her servants fanning her with feathers like this one. So it's a fan, not a dust mop.

Her mother continues, "You know we will all catch our deaths if you continue stirring up this bad air, Elisabetta."

Bethy II lays the duster down beside me, close enough that I can more keenly examine feathers that look to be plucked from an actual Big Bird. And I got to see up close and personal how ostriches are a real thing here. Then, of course, there's Leonardo's ostrich egg globe.

Who owned the bird that wore these feathers, and do they regrow? I marvel, staring at the low-tech feathered air conditioner. It's the only obsession that makes sense to my addled brain.

But having said brain affixed like this on trivia is keeping me from thinking straight. *"Achoo!"* I think I must be allergic to something in the room.

"Alla salute!" the women exclaim in unison. Somewhere nearby, Wilbur, the adorable little piglet I rescued from the fate of being turned into a pre-Lenten feast for Lorenzo de' Medici and his hundreds of expected dinner guests, grunts.

"She's been a little strange," Bethy chimes in, pointing to her head.

My newly unleashed-by-reason mind still streams irrelevantly, but my eyes begin to focus well enough to see that Bethy appears quite the modern schoolgirl, wearing my backpack and sporting my earbuds.

Weirdly, she's picked up the fan and begins to shake it side to side, bobbing her head in time to something coming through those earbuds. What—or who—she's listening to is beyond me, but suffice it to say, it's probably not the Retro Pigs. Not the way she's got Wilbur sitting on her lap, so that when she isn't busy waving that fan, she's dunking her fingers in what looks to be milk—unpasteurized, of course, because Louis

Pasteur, who created the system to sterilize and kill bacteria and germs found in raw milk, won't even be born for another three hundred years or so—in a funky, antique blue-and-white pitcher on top of one of the expensive ivory-inlaid black walnut tables . . . and allowing Wilbur to suck milk off her pinky. And giggling.

I sit up in a hurry, wondering if a persistent memory of seeing my mom talking to Kairos isn't just the remnant of some bad dream, when Bethy II stops and nudges Wilbur, squealing, to the floor.

"What are you doing, Elisabetta?!" What else of mine could she have misappropriated (definition: steal for reals)?

"Do not worry yourself, Carlotta. Your mamma is in good hands. I have been your ears for her," she says, pulling out the earbuds.

"My ears! For Mamma—what are you talking about?"

"*La musica!* You fainted away before the bell tower on the Duomo struck two."

As she's speaking, I can hear the church bells chiming the half hour. So I was out for a good thirty minutes.

"Lucky for your mother, Kairos was able to find her help. '*A doctorrr in di 'ousa, a doctorrr in di 'ousa,*' he was calling!" I have to smile at Bethy II's attempts at recreating the English phrase she must've heard through the earbuds.

"And a *chirurgo alla Palazzo* then was able to cure your mamma. It was frightening, the needle he stabbed her arm with! But she's breathing *encorro.*" As she delivers this news, Wilbur grunts and snorts, trying to find his way back onto Bethy's lap.

What is she describing? A shot? They gave Mamma a shot? This would seem to confirm my worst fears. "Breathing again—was she—?! Where is she? I WANT MY MOTHER!"

It's like I'm speaking Greek. No one pays my words the slightest attention. They are all glued to the tablet as Bethy stabs the screen with

her milky finger. I grab my tablet to see what everyone is looking at.

"That looks to be the Palazzo Pitti," Bethy says, inspecting the setting behind my mother.

"*Si,*" says Signora Vincenzo. "From what Elisabetta tells me, we are the ones called upon to protect you from misfortune. *La bella fortuna* is on your side, Carlotta." Putting an arm around me, she attempts a consoling smile that looks more like a grimace.

I squirm out of her embrace and examine my tablet, hoping against hope the scene from the other side is still visible.

But *la donna* Vincenzo continues to hold my arm, intent on getting credit for her display of heroism in resuscitating me. "When my cousin Viola came running on the news from my Elisabetta that you were lying on the floor, suffering from the hysteria, I hied my way pronto here to the palazzo."

Wilbur nudges her around the ankles. "Who is going to take this runt home, Elisabetta? And how will we feed yet another mouth until this one is grown and fit for slaughter?"

At this, Wilbur runs a circle underneath the sofa and out between Signora Vincenzo's legs, almost toppling that formidable *donna* in the process.

Signora Vincenzo kicks him away unceremoniously and turns to me with what I can only guess are fake tears in her eyes. "Carlotta, this news has pulled at *mio cuore!*"

A cast-iron heart, in my experience.

Until that Viola woman chimes in. "You are fools! With the French king close and a battle imminent, if said king were to capture this girl, and *Magnifico* to find his servant girl has been ransomed—"

"Servant! Me? Ransomed!" My tangled brain isn't sure which threat to find more horrifying.

"A king's ransom," nods Signora Vincenzo, embracing me now with newfound devotion.

"Not to mention the attentions of the Pope! As the good Fra Savonarola warns us, 'Beware of those without faith,'" Viola continues. "'We weep even for such infidels,' as the girl before us!"

The Pope! I think hard: Is this the time of the Inquisition in Rome?!

"But Carlotta is no infidel!" cries Bethy II in my defense.

But Viola's just getting started. "She attracts the wrong attentions. Savonarola himself has denounced the appearance of *una strega* in our midst. Don't you see? The omens she foretells with her magic tablet— flying machines, future events . . ."

They think I'm a witch!

". . . as Leonardo himself shared with *il Magnifico* by way of warning!"

"Hold on, this doesn't seem right!" I cry out. "Leonardo surely wouldn't—"

"Then Lorenzo, in turn, implored Savonarola to reverse her

prophecy to save himself from death."

"Me? Why would I want Lorenzo to die?" I implore, before remembering with a sinking heart that I had told Leonardo that this would be the year of *il Magnifico*'s death.

"And so it is . . . this witch casts her spell, and if her magic were to fall into the hands of the French, or worse, Pope Innocent through his spies, as some claim they have foreseen . . ."

A witch . . . a *witch*, they think I'm a witch! I can't get past that word! What did they do to women accused of witchcraft during the Inquisition? My brain's on fire trying to think my way through what this accusation could presage (definition: predict).

"Viola, surely you cannot believe the wagging tongues of the court," objects Signora Vincenzo, squeezing my shoulders. "She may be strange, but she brings no harm."

Vaguely, I wonder why the innkeeper's wife is suddenly being so kind.

"It isn't what you think, cousin," says Bethy II. "She is wise about useless things, but when it comes to affairs of the heart—"

"At least I don't go chasing after every boy under the sun!" I can't help but bite back.

"The secret to her knowing is no mystery, though," Bethy says, as she grabs the tablet out of my hands.

"Bethy, no!" I scream, jumping up in panic. "Ooh, my ankle!" I feel my legs crumple again. Bethy catches me mid-fall.

"There, proof!" Viola exclaims. "She suffers for these crimes."

"Nonsense, Viola. She hurt her ankle coming to the tavern." Signora Vincenzo glares at her cousin. "Here, Carlotta, I brought something suitable for your feet too." She pushes me down on the sofa, trying to shove my swollen foot into a peasant-style boot.

"*Youch!* You're hurting me!" I yell.

Apparently, this cry translates as distress in any and all languages because she stops shoving and allows me to pull the boot gently over my wounded ankle.

Again, Wilbur shows his snout, this time right under my foot. "Oh!" I cry, almost in tears. It's all too much!

"Shoo! Elisabetta, you'd best squirrel away this little pest before *il Magnifico* turns this sow into soap!" Viola scolds.

Sow! So Wilbur's a girl? Before this can register, *la donna* Viola turns her wagging finger back on me.

"And you! You will be punished—Lorenzo de' Medici will not stand for his home being defiled so, thoughtless girl! Bringing pigs into this palazzo!"

Trying hard not to respond to the scold with something I will regret

saying later, I busy myself pulling on the second boot. At least they'll give me a little more support, I think, once the hard part is over.

I carefully swing my leg out to admire Italy's finest. After all, the Italians are known for their leather, are they not? Hand-sewn. Soft. The style's sort of like a cross between a lace-up moccasin and a bootie. Not horrible, I think, though I'm quite sure *my* Bethy wouldn't be caught dead in them. Side lacing, little fringy thing design-wise, leather sole—wouldn't help much on cobblestones, but still. Beats my flimsy slippers or those horrifyingly stilt-like chopines that I have seen on a few supposedly fashionable Florentine women tottering around the cobblestones. Talk about your accident waiting to happen! These are high heels in the middle, where the platform comes under your sole and arches up toward the heel.

I mean, could you see *me* attempting *that* balancing act?!

Come to think of it, maybe I already am. . . .

II.
Sorting Out Contradictions!

I complain to Bethy about needing to go to the bathroom-loo-WC-whatever they call it here. I mean, when a girl's gotta go, a girl's gotta go!

She points me to what is, literally, a closet down the hall where there's a marble bench that has a large hole in it (and who knows what's on the underside to catch the waste!), woolen towels to wipe, and a table with a washbasin and a pitcher filled with water. Stinks like too much perfume to mask bad B.O.

I wonder if I should squat, like Mamma's always saying you should do in public bathrooms. I mean, here they've gone through plagues, the pox, chlamydia (we had to study STDs in health class this year, and luckily, Mamma made me get the HPV vaccine, 'cause whoever would've imagined *this* scenario) . . . and who knows what else!

I try for the squat, but after a moment I realize that, for one thing, squatting on one foot is nearly impossible, and for another, I'm alone here, in private. I let go of any notion of delicacy I initially felt around this situation. For once, I'm glad I don't have to worry about female troubles of the monthly variety—I shudder to think of what options are available in this day and age for managing all that.

At first, it feels weird to bare my tush on the cold marble, but ultimately, I find it's more about trying not to fall in. Since I stashed my phone in my pocket, I can check my messages and maybe update the blog without many eyes watching my every move. They seem to be getting way too interested in my electronics. Besides, who knows the next time I might have this luxury without spies angling for evidence of my so-called witchy ways!

Truth is, I need breathing room. Whatever mess I've gotten myself into with this stupid time travel experiment—and whose idea was that?!—I need a way to process. And writing's always been my way to do that.

As soon as I log in to the blog, I notice a comment . . . Billy's!

submitted on 2018/04/12 at 4:10 p.m. comment by Billy V.:

> Charley, the kids are going crazy here: Lex gave some cockamamie story about you two in the garage predicting his baseball future and thinks he's gonna be fingered in a missing-person story and Beth's pretending she can't be bothered but I know deep down she's worried, and basically, I don't know what to tell them. That you've actually met the real Leonardo da Vinci? Like anyone's gonna believe me!
>
> Guessing to get you back here in time the 2nd golden compass is gonna be important. You still have #1, right? Gotta figure out how to teleport #2.
>
> BTW, hard to read your posts—they seem to fade as soon as I open the Web page. Gotta save screenshots to read.
>
> Anyways, I biked over to your house to tell your dad . . . something . . . and no one was home. Luckily. 'Cause honestly, your dad's gonna be so salty . . . and he's gonna

wanna know stuff I can't tell him, like how we got the stupid formula! But I left him a sticky note on his computer where I'm sure he'll see it.

P.S. U say u saw & heard your mom? Like a streaming video or something? In ur next post, pls explain how/what. Could use something like that in my new virtual world: Leonardo's War Games.

P.P.S. Also, take pix 4 me: catapults, swords, cannons, armor, soldiers. This is gonna be awesome.

Well then! Bethy's worried about me . . . fat chance. Lex is worried about his star baseball future with the Washington Nationals, and even Billy seems mostly concerned about my bringing back images for his new video game. Some friends! But I need them now if I needed them ever, because this new threat—witchcraft—sounds serious.

Blog Entry #5. FYEO. March 8—Carnival time?

Beginning to think time makes no difference. At least not time as we think of it. The campanile of the Duomo strikes here—hour, quarter hour, half hour. Another clock on a different church—an alley and a sculpture-filled piazza away— chimes the same hour, quarter hour, half hour, but starts and ends moments later. The net effect is that some clock somewhere is almost always sounding off. It is total cacophony.

I think I'm obsessed with time because I am SOOO out of it. But then, somehow I can see you through time—and

Mamma, and even Kairos, who seems to be literally every-where at the same time—but you are in a different space-time plane, going about your day, same as always. Mind-blowing.

This place is nuts. Their so-called Republic is really anarchy! Rules make no sense—pigs running around palace floors. Il Magnifico's like an oligarch. The pope may be on a witch hunt—for me!

Urgently in need of key that reverses Kairos's time travel formula. And a super-duper battery, or death may be my destiny here. Any hints on speeding the process of fission from radioactive decay, for example? Sun power from here insufficient.

I think you're onto something with the other golden compass. There's got to be a way to teleport to my time zone now. Think it may take two to un-tango the complications of massive temporal dislocation.

Your Partner in Time Travel (a.k.a. PITT)

As I hit send, the now-familiar specter of other-time voices seeps through the phone. This time, Dad.

"Yes, thanks for letting me know. No, I did *not* know anyone hacked into the system."

Hackers? Would that mean me and Billy?

I open the video chat to see if there's video with the sound. Dad's standing in the garage, looking more than a little forlorn. His workshop's a total mess—like a tornado's torn through there. I guess the energy transmission that created momentum for my trip out of that world stirred up quite a bit of dust. I can see what remains of our time machine behind him on the workbench. Not a pretty sight.

"What I do know is my daughter has vanished into thin air, which apparently has to do with a boy and a school project, and my wife is going to—"

This news is both scary and hopeful. Scary, 'cause I'm gonna be in BIG TROUBLE if I ever get home alive. Hopeful, 'cause even if I am grounded for the rest of my life (which I think I might happily agree to at this moment), it can't be nearly as bad as being burned at the stake. No, but seriously—!

"What's that, Viola?" Dad asks.

Viola! *Impossibile*. Too many coincidences here—Elisabetta and Beth; Alessandro and Lex; the Vincenzos; and now *another* Viola—it's creepy. Would these have already been disturbances in the space-time continuum if I hadn't jumped the veil, so to speak?

"I don't know of any video games that would open spontaneously on that computer. *No one* is to touch any of the secure files on Operation Firenze. Let me check the remote network interface. Yes, hold on. . . ."

Dad sets his phone down while he goes over to the banks of remote servers, which are the backup for the very Top Secret Operation Firenze program from his work that I have somehow hitchhiked back in time on. They seem to be doing their usual blinking and beeping. Nothing seems amiss besides the mess, and I think we're in the clear until Dad gets that puzzled/angry look on his face that he gets when he's trying to decide if I'm in trouble. He mumbles something about a bug in the system and shakes his head as he picks his phone up.

"No need to call the police, Viola. I have a feeling it's no more mysterious than a science fair experiment run amok. . . . Um-hmm. Yes, I get it—protocol. Sure, I will definitely file the report on this. Thanks, Viola. You bet my daughter will be answering to me on this one . . ."

I see him hang up the phone and plop down on his bench, looking dejected.

"... as soon as I find her."

Someone's knocking, bringing me back to the present—this other present.

"*Carlotta? Ci sei caduta dentro?*"

I clap on the Translator. "No, I did not fall in, Elisabetta."

"Good thing, because *il Magnifico* is screaming and cursing."

Probably demanding my head. "I think I'll stay in here then, *grazie*."

"But Leonardo, he also calls for you."

Reluctantly, I pocket my phone once more and emerge from the WC gloomily imagining what it will feel like to walk to the gallows or, worse, be burned at the stake. At least death by decapitation is instantaneous.

Bethy II understands none of my predicament, of course. As she leads me down the long hall to where the Masters of the Renaissance are no doubt waiting to pronounce judgment on one less-than-masterful girl, she natters on about her complicated love life. As if such girl talk still mattered. And yet, as my only girl friend here, I am beginning to treasure her confidences. In a strange way, she makes me feel more like a girl who belongs.

"Oh, but you know Sandro is a man of faith, not war! Though he promised, his vows to the Church mean nothing. He has pledged we will consummate our love when next he visits."

Despite myself, I can't help but be a bit shocked by this admission. "And he's a priest? But the whole celibacy thing ... that doesn't bug you? And you're like ready, you know, to sleep with him?!"

"Sleep? What has sleep to do with love?"

"Well, I mean, not exactly sleeping but, well, like, do you already know him well enough to ..."

"*O, si.* I have known Sandro since we were but children hanging around the stables."

Whoa, talk about paradoxes! They demand strict adherence to the rules, except for the exceptions. Priests have girlfriends. They boast great advances in education but intolerance for new ideas. Extreme wealth side by side with extreme poverty. A flowering of art and beauty, along with enough ugliness of spirit to destroy it.

In the midst of all that, it's even more of a wonder that Leonardo could emerge with his superpowers for art, invention, music, engineering, science, math . . . and I thought pursuing the whole "Renaissance girl, master of learning" thing was tough for *me*!

But Bethy II here seems to find no contradiction in the idea that her boyfriend could be a priest, or cardinal, or whatever.

"So then what's the deal with the old dude?"

"Massimo? It is so complicated, Carlotta. My father's health is failing. He can no longer work and cannot pay the loans he owes the de' Medicis for our purchase of the *taverna*. It would take a lifetime for a tenant farmer like my father to save up his own money—or make enough from the few florins we earn from lodgers—to buy what must sustain our family! Ser Massimo has offered to pay off our family's debt in exchange for my hand. It was the only way we could keep our lodgings here in Firenze. If I do not accept his hand, my sisters and I will be sent to a convent and my parents will be left with nothing. I cannot allow *mio padre* to die dishonored."

That's a sad story. "Sorry, Bethy. I bet your dad's gonna get better!"

When I look up at her, Bethy's got a big, fat smile on her face. "*Si*. It will help *mio padre* to be rid of this burden. And I will still be allowed to see my beloved when he returns with Cardinal Giulio!"

The whole husband-father-boyfriend thing still doesn't sit right with me, but I have to admire Bethy's family loyalty, and her concern for her dad. Especially under the circumstances. Especially since I may have screwed up my own dad's life, big-time.

"Tough choices, for sure," I concur, shaking my head. "And I thought giving up Facebook time to practice my music was a sacrifice. What you're doing is amazeballs, Bethy."

"Face book? *Uno volto folio?* Oh, how I wish I were lettered, that I could understand these things!"

The hallway turns and we are walking past what has to be a kitchen, 'cause I can feel heat from the ovens, and whatever's cooking smells so *delizioso*, it sets my tummy a-rumble.

"Say, Bethy, I know they're like, expecting us ASAP and everything, but do you think the kitchen here could whip me up, maybe, a pizza? I'm really hungry!"

Bethy looks quizzical. *"Questo pizza?"*

"Aww, man! Don't tell me you don't even have any pepperoni in Italy yet! *Mozzarella?*"

"Ah, certo, il formaggio. Un momento. We must await a time when *il cuoco* has gone to market. Cook does not permit strangers in his kitchen."

Seems like Florence's openness in this age of rebirth may not extend past its riverbanks.

We arrive back in the grand salon, but *il Magnifico* and Leonardo are nowhere in sight. Neither, for that matter, are Signora Vincenzo and Viola. Nor is there any sign of little Wilbur.

"So what's the deal here, Bethy? You yank me from my private sanctuary—to wait?"

"Oh no! Kairos assured me that they would be here!"

"Kairos is . . . *here*?" Last I could conjure, he was in modern-day Firenze reviving my mom, who, I pray with all my heart, isn't dying.

"Naturalmente, no!" she replies. *"È qui."* She reaches for my tablet, which I had stashed under my backpack, and opens the cover.

I grab it from her, and there is Billy's face. Before I can yell at Bethy to stop being so nosy, I am absorbed into a different drama.

Billy's in his room. I can hear music playing in the background. Sounds like a Simon and Garfunkel tune. Figures he'd be listening to oldies. I hear him reciting the lyrics with my name, "For Charley, whenever I may find her. Whenever I may find her. Whenever I may find her," almost like a mantra. It's touching, really. And reassuring.

He's got his tablet open on his bed to TeenWords and he keeps checking, like he's waiting. I realize it's my turn to play, so I toggle to the app and type: POSITIONFIRENZE. He plays the word ANNO, to which I append MCDXCII.

"I know, Charley. I get it. I need specifics!" I hear him say before I see his next move pop up: COORDINATE. I toggle back to the video chat screen and—whoa, people: Billy has left the room!

III.
The Waiting Game

Bethy's been sitting way too close to me on the sofa. Contrary to how it looks, the seat is hard and scratchy. I scoot away from her, trying to create a more comfortable distance.

"This is Lex?" she asks, perplexed, as I flip through my Facebook story. I guess to her eyes, Billy, with his glasses, braces, and serious expression, looks like no great prize.

"Oh, no, that's my friend Billy. We study together. He's working with me on the science project that got me here."

"Studying? You—a girl?"

"So what? I'm a girl, you're a girl. I happen to be a girl who's good at science and, like, inventing things." I get defensive when I hear this, 'cause even now, I mean, even five hundred years from now, it's kind of assumed girls can't do science or technology. Not true!

"*Questo sci-ence?*"

"What do you mean? Science is how we understand the world through observing it, and then proving those observations through experimentation."

I can see this explanation goes right over her head. "You know, Ser Leonardo practically invented science! 'To see is to know,' and all that?"

"It's just that . . . I wish I could study."

"I could teach you!"

"Oh no, that would not be right! Massimo would never approve of this!"

I can't help but feel exasperated: Why is it that girls' brains at our age turn to mush? I mean, like, literally: The ability of a teenager to focus on the really important stuff—like building a time machine, say—seems to take a hit when members of the opposite sex are involved. Honestly, I almost fell victim to this heart-in-my-head syndrome yesterday. But for a time machine, my mind might well be mush now too.

While we're waiting for the Florentine VIPs to show, maybe I can teach Bethy a bit. Thinking it's gonna require major help from Translator. "C'mere," I say, and again pat the cushion next to me on the sofa.

Bethy again scooches close, excited for another look at the tablet.

"How does it contain the whole world, Carlotta—your magic box?"

"Well, Elisabetta, as I mentioned, this is Facebook," I say in my best teaching voice as I show her the app. "*Volto folio*, you would call it. It's a place I can write notes about what I'm doing, find out what my friends are up to, and post pictures, see?" I turn the tablet around, put an arm around Bethy to bring her in close enough to the frame, and snap a photo of us talking.

"*Mamma mia!*" she exclaims, stroking her face as if to make sure it's still attached when I show her the photo. "You have captured such a likeness—you and me?"

"Yep. You and me." She can't seem to pull her eyes off the screen. "And this is how we're going to post the picture on Facebook . . . where maybe, someday, my friends will see it." I type in the words while reciting my update, "*Due regazze a Firenze:* Elisabetta and me."

I am able to upload the selfie, but I have no idea if it will actually post.

"*Posta,*" she repeats. "*Come una lettura?*"

"Yes, like a letter. Can't you read? *Leggere?*" She gives me that blank stare again and it hits me, of course she can't read! "I can see I've got a lot of work to do here to get you up to speed!"

My heart skips at the thought. Maybe I can help someone here; maybe it's not just my impossible quest to learn everything, but also to share what I know that has drawn me here.

"*Ah, si!* Sandro knows his letters. He would be so impressed to see that I have become lettered as well!"

I scan my brain to think whether any of the books I have on my Kindle app might be good primers. And as soon as the word "primer" flashes in my mind, it hits me that when I was writing my essay last quarter on how public education in America got started, I downloaded a copy of a McGuffey Reader. Even though all the parental buzz in my neck of the woods is how digital media is disrupting the hard-won mental wiring that we humans have evolved since Gutenberg, I'd still start her on the written word. Electronically speaking. The reader is in English, of course, but I consider this a good thing: Reading + English = Bethy II's ticket to the future. Plus, it's got lots of pictures.

Back to Facebook. I'm scrolling down the page when Bethy dramatically puts her hand over the screen.

"Who is this?" A weird dreamy look comes over her face, and I have to pry her palm back to even see what she's looking at.

"That, Bethy, is Lex. The kid who is definitely NOT my boyfriend."

"*Lex-y*, of course! I see he is very . . . *hot*, you say?"

I decide to keep scrolling down the timeline. No sense in focusing on the boy who got me into this mess. 'Cause he sure as heck isn't getting me out of it!

We've come to the photos from Dad's office now. The one I managed to snap of my dad in the elevator before he abandoned me during Take Your Child to Work Day. That picture got 126 likes and 10 comments—and this from Beth: "Whatdya you do this time to make your dad so mad?" Better question: Why's Beth acting so gnarly? I trace my finger wistfully over Dad's face, wishing I could feel the rough stubble on his chin.

"And the signor, he is *tua padre*, Carlotta?"

"*Si*," I whisper wistfully. Oh, Dad, are you looking for me?

And then I hear a ding letting me know there's a new entry on TeenWords. Billy's next play: "Meet@midnight."

Wow, that's *so* weird. It should've been my move! But before I even get the chance to think about what it might mean, Bethy's punching me in the arm and shushing me excitedly.

"Oww, that hurts!" I abruptly let go of the tablet to push her hands away; it wedges between the cushions.

"Shh! It is *il Magnifico* himself. He mustn't find you here."

"*Questo?*" I ask, but she's motioning at the door, and I hear footsteps rapidly approaching.

From outside the door to our salon we hear Lorenzo loudly cursing, "That dishonorable da Vinci!" and then further cursing about how Leonardo's word means nothing, nor will Lorenzo pay his commission.

Elisabetta slips into panic mode. "Pronto, Carlotta! You must hide!" she says, shoving me off the sofa, and I once again find myself on my tush. "Ser Leonardo will kill me if anything ill becomes of you! And *il Magnifico* will kill us both if he finds you here!"

"What the heck, Bethy?!" I exclaim as I pick myself up off the floor.

She's stopped noticing me. She's lifting the heavy tapestry that covers a wall facing us, nervously tapping across the wall's midpoint. As she disappears under the tapestry, I hear a hollow echo.

"*Viene, Carlotta,*" she hisses at me, and, like in one of those old Hollywood suspense movies, a panel slowly creaks open. "*Il Magnifico* cannot find you here. He will recognize *la strega* from the piazza."

I open my mouth to ask her how she knows about what happened earlier with Leonardo.

Bethy places a finger against my lips. "*Silenzio!* You will be safer in there." She points to the opening. "Now, go!"

I squish through the panel as Bethy pushes it shut. My heart is racing. The tablet! It's wedged halfway in between the cushions of the couch, and showing who knows what mysteries. I know I need to be still as a mouse, but if Signor Lorenzo sees it again . . ."

It's really dark and stuffy in the narrow hallway here. I feel all kinds of webs and imagine little crawly things climbing up my legs. Good thing I'm no arachnophobe (definition: someone who is scared of spiders). But bats are a different story. I wonder if there's a word for that.

And dust! I catch my nose before a sneeze can blow my cover.

Cursing loudly, Lorenzo has stormed into the grand *sala*, the room I just left.

"Bring me that laggard Leonardo!"

Why the great Lorenzo de' Medici would be yelling to Bethy—it doesn't seem fair.

"The maestro is late with his commission, as usual. And this one, a matter of life and death for the Republic."

Elisabetta's muffled voice comes across like a cat's purr. *"Mi scusi, Magnifico."*

I pace back and forth on tippy toe, nervous that Lorenzo will come across my screen again. He's already proclaimed it "magic" and me, apparently, a sorceress for conjuring it. In the dark, I pace my face right into a musty stash of stuff and feel the urge to sneeze again. I use the hem of my ugly dress to muffle my sneeze. Feeling my way into that narrow crawl space, I dimly detect a deep shelf storing ancient treasures, and find myself staring at an unfinished marble bust of none other than Lorenzo the Magnificent himself. No doubt a treasure that future generations will revere as a fine example of Renaissance sculpture. A giant wooden picture frame, carved within an inch of its life and undoubtedly meant to hold a Renaissance masterpiece, is crammed into a cubby next to it. I thrill to think that it might one day hold a painting by Michelangelo or Raphael . . . or Leonardo da Vinci himself.

Lorenzo's voice booms out. "Well, go find him for me, girl. Pronto!"

Bethy answers loudly—I'm guessing for my benefit. "Good signor! I would not know where to find the artist. I am but the cleaning girl, here to scrub the salon ahead of the reception for *Magnifico's* most esteemed guests. You will recall that tonight is the masquerade ball at the Palazzo?"

I wish there was a peephole so I could see what was happening in the silence that follows.

"Eh? Carnevale?" Lorenzo halts, as if the big celebration had, indeed, slipped his mind. "A masquerade ball? Do not be foolish, *ragazza!* Of course I haven't forgotten my own damnable celebration!"

Bethy squeaks something I can't quite make out.

Something clatters, like a hammer on stone, pounding so close it startles me. My heart's about to jump out of my chest.

"NO ONE DENIES *Magnifico*, do you hear me, girl? Get me da Vinci!"

"*Achoo!*" I sneeze and immediately pinch my nose to stave off another.

"*Achoo!*" I hear echoed back. Did Bethy fake one to cover for me?

"*Salute,*" Lorenzo responds.

"*Molte grazie.* If it pleases you, *Magnifico*, I can run for a messenger to see if the maestro can be found."

Another momentary silence. When at last he speaks, Lorenzo's voice has softened.

"*Scusa, ragazza.* Of course you are not the maestro's keeper. No one is! Apparently, even I, the ruler of Florence, have little authority over that man! He possesses a golden touch, but his word is worth no more than tin."

"*Si, Magnifico.* The touch of gold . . . ," Bethy murmurs, even as I hear her banging something hard against the wall near my head.

"Stop pounding, you crazy girl! You disturb the newest of my paintings by Sandro Botticelli!"

Botticelli. Little Barrel. One of the most important artists of Renaissance Florence, I recall. Hanging just here on the other side of the wall.

"I mean no harm, *Magnifico*," Beth responds loudly. A warning to me perhaps? "You were saying about Ser Leonardo?"

"Ah, yes. The engineer. His promise means nothing. But this commission is critical, for it centers on the security of the Republic—now that the sour breath of the French king and his men begin an assault against Florence!"

The hammer of a fist again, this time perilously close to my ear. Startled, I bounce up in the murky darkness and bang my head against a low ceiling, hitting my shoulder against the wall on my way down.

"Damn it, Charley!" I yell, setting off a commotion. Just as Newton's third law of motion predicts, there is an equal and opposite reaction on the other side of the wall. The vibration set off by my body—an unstoppable force—crashing against the wall—an immovable object—causes a tremor that reverberates through the walls.

Lorenzo himself yells, *"Non, la* Primavera!"

La Primavera. I conjure an image in my mind of the famous depiction of lots of beautiful and, at least to my eyes, even some quite pregnant women, in Botticelli's famous tableau.

Bethy shrieks, *"O Dio!* I have it. Fear not!" I picture her jumping up with the spring of a gymnast onto the sofa, attempting to steady the masterpiece.

"You will pay, *regazza,* should my treasure be ripped from the wall!" *il Magnifico* exclaims.

At that moment, I hear crackling audio just outside my hiding space. My tablet!

But Bethy brazenly continues her playacting. I guess she's heard it too. *"Prego, Magnifico,* methinks there are MISCHIEVOUS VERMIN."

Another loud crackling noise that can only be electronic. How can that even be?

Bethy pounds the wall again. "These pests nibble at your tapestries, *Magnifico!"*

Lorenzo pounces on her. "Girl, I told you . . . continue to shake the walls with such reverberations and you will severely regret when the painting falls."

I shuffle my feet and squeak in what I hope sounds like a mouse.

"Esci, ratti!" Bethy shouts.

"Questo? Rats behind these walls? I will kill the filthy vermin!"

Bethy squeaks something incomprehensible to cover up another crackle from my phone. What the heck? I thought I turned off the sound after . . . unless . . .

"My priceless tapestries . . . not to mention their known affinity to biting, and here, just beneath the nursery," Lorenzo sputters on, "where my grandsire and namesake, Lorenzo, lies tenderly sleeping in his gilded cradle!"

Humph. He should be worried about how rats and gerbils are known to carry the bacteria that cause death from the plague. But then I remember: It's way too soon for anyone to understand about how infectious diseases are spread.

"Perhaps *uno gatto* can solve *Magnifico's* pest problem."

A cat, or a pig, I think, suddenly wondering where Wilbur's gotten to. My musing is interrupted by a crackling noise that's disturbingly twenty-first century.

"Wait! What is this?" Lorenzo asks. And without even seeing where his eyes are going, I know in my bones that he's spied my tablet.

I'm dead.

"Carolina's *tavoletta*, *Magnifico*. *La bambina*—do you recall the girl in the piazza? It holds the drawing of Leonardo's wondrous cannon design," Bethy reminds him.

"Why do you distract me, girl; Leonardo is the one I seek. And his cannon . . ."

I hear Bethy begging for her life. "*Si, Magnifico*, it is indeed Leonardo of whom you have been speaking! I . . . I will run for him, pronto. Please, whatever punishment—"

"Yes, run, impudent girl! I have far more important matters to worry about."

With that, I hear Lorenzo's footsteps fading. Finally, I can breathe.

As I slowly stand up from my crouched position, I can feel my fingers and toes tingling.

"*Psst*, Carlotta!" Bethy hisses loudly. "*Vieni!* You are safe."

Cautiously, I rise, feeling my way back along the wall toward what I hope is the secret panel door opening. Now that my pounding heart is settling into a more regular rhythm, I wonder at the carelessly piled knickknacks and whatnots awash in dust mites and cobwebs: a few books—folios, I guess—consigned to history's dustbin. Literally.

Because, if I remember right, Gutenberg's printing press was just invented, like, yesterday. And Leonardo da Vinci came up with a design that improved on it. Naturally.

Priceless treasures in my world, I think, running my fingers across the leather spines illumined with Latin titles embossed in gold letters. Especially since that strictatarian Dominican Cardinal Savonarola, who thought beauty was sinful and started the bonfires of the vanities to burn books, jewels, art, and furs back in the day, also decried the wisdom in books as evil and burned them to stop the flow of knowledge.

Censoring books has a long history, but art? I remember hearing

APPLICATION DE LA PRESSE D'IMPRIMERIE

PRINTING PRESS

ANWENDUNG DER DRUCKERPRESSE

UN PERFEZIONAMENTO DELLA PRESSA DA STAMPA

not that long ago about a rich art collector in my day who thought a drawing he bought at auction might be an original Leonardo, *La Bella Principessa*. He was on an international hunt to find out whether the portrait on vellum he found could be a real-live Leonardo. His theory: *The Beautiful Princess* might be an illustration for a royal wedding book. If it proved out, his $20,000 investment would be worth $80 million instead!

And here I stand amidst a trove of possible treasures! My fingers itch to inspect one—or better yet, pocket one to carry home. If home I may someday go.

"*Carlotta! Dove stai andando?*"

Where am I? Bethy's voice pulls me back into the present, pounding on the wall to guide me to the exact spot of the panel.

I push, thinking the hidden door must swing open, putting all my weight against it where her taps are loudest. The wall opens up and I fall into the gilded room that gleams so brightly—flickering with candlelight, chandeliers, and sconces—that it hurts my eyes.

Bethy reaches out a hand to pull me out.

"Bethy!" I can't help but hug her hard. "My hero!"

"*Io non sono un'eroina!*" she replies. "It is my own life I fear for: Leonardo would kill me if any harm were to come to you!"

"Leonardo! Is he here?"

"Soon. Meanwhile, you see, I have protected your treasure." With that, she pulls the tablet out from its hiding place under the cushions.

"*Più voci,*" she says, pointing to the screen.

"More voices?" I ask.

"*Tua Bee-ly.*" Then I actually see Elisabetta blush. "*E Lex.*"

IV.
TeenWords

Sure enough, it seems my pals are (virtually) in the room.

"Okay, Webhead. I gotta come clean here. I was, uh, kinda *kissing* Charley when she disappeared," Lex says.

Could this get any more embarrassing? I pray Lex's true confessions stop there.

"I couldn't say it in front of Beth 'cause, you know. Beth's *totally* into me, and I don't want to hurt her feelings. But something so *mysterious* happened to Charley, and I'm afraid it's really bad, like that stupid contraption dematerialized her."

I see Billy's face crumple. "Geez, Lex. Whattaya gotta tell me that for? *Kissing.* As if things aren't bad enough."

They're sitting in Billy's room—Lex is sprawled out on top of Billy's bed, while Billy remains ever watchful at his desk with every electronic gadget known to mankind open and running. I can hear music, texts, messages, and random beeps. Such a geek!

Lex sits up, suddenly curious. "Um . . . *you like,* I mean, LIKE Charley?"

Billy makes an inscrutable face. "She's my best friend, Lex. And if you cared anything about her, you'd be more worried about finding her in one piece than a stupid kiss that never happened."

What is he talking about? And why did my heart just skip a beat?

Billy's always been an open book to me and I never would've guessed, not in a million years. Because if he really has a crush . . . and given the heroic efforts he's going through to help me figure this all out . . . my heart says—I can't go there.

To change the subject, I decide to answer Billy's last TeenWords play: NOGPS. It's a miracle when I hear it ping on his computer.

On hearing the ping, Lex gets up and stares into Billy's screen. As he reads, his brow furrows, his mouth drops, and finally, he blurts out, "NOGPS? That's not a word! Wait a sec, Billy—who're you playing there?"

Billy pings back: ASKLEO.

"Charley."

"Ha ha. Didn't know you had a sense of humor, Webhead."

Elisabetta's watching over my shoulder intently. She lets out a wolf whistle. "*Si calda!* Lex is so *'ot!*"

"*Hot,*" I correct her. "We pronounce the *h*. Like ha-ha."

"Ah-ah," she repeats.

I can see Billy's trying to be detached about the kiss. "Suit yourself, Lex."

Lex watches a second more. "No joke? She's okay? Then I don't really need to worry that I disappeared her. And you told her dad and everything?"

"What are they saying, Carlotta?" Bethy's obviously dying to know. "Why is it so loud, and how is it that this room is lit up like fireflies? Where are the torches?"

Lex is still intent on figuring out what's going on. "So where the heck is she anyway, Billy? And who's this Leo dude?"

"*Questo?*" Bethy's mouth is agape.

Before I can translate, Billy stares longingly straight at his screen, straight into my heart, as he responds to Lex.

"Florence, Italy. Charley's found her da Vinci."

As Lex's face turns from relief to astonishment, I send a new TeenWords play, hitting enter three times to be sure: PALAZZO VECCHIO XIIAM.

V.

No Charley Left Behind

The screen goes blank and my heart drops. I check to see if I can reboot the tablet. Billy's gotta get that message 'cause I am for sure running out of time!

Footsteps entering the hallway. Did Lorenzo come back? Should I hide again? I fire a look at Bethy, prepared to make a dash for it.

But then, a friendly voice. "Carlotta, I am here at your command. And I desire to understand . . . everything!"

Leonardo is in the room!

"Where were you, maestro?" Bethy asks. "*Magnifico* was looking for you!"

"*Si*. Of course. I am not quite ready to unveil my latest invention for night battle. I must complete the experiment under the next full moon so as not to imperil the likes of Carlotta—or the next of her kind to appear. *Il Magnifico* will have to wait."

I can tell Leo's more into the art of art than the art of war. Every time he talks about this night battle commission for Lorenzo, he gets the same distasteful look on his face. Like, it's just a paycheck. I myself am hoping to avoid that working for "just a paycheck" trap once I grow up.

Which, for me, means mastering time travel, among other innovations.

But first, I have to figure out how to time travel home in time to help Mamma *and* for the science fair, 'cause if I don't win that, no doubt I will be getting left behind. That's why bringing Leo up to speed on twenty-first-century science and tech is gonna be my greatest challenge.

"So, get this, Leo. I need a lot of power to activate the time machine from here." I wonder briefly about how I'm gonna get ahold of the second key that Billy's got in his possession, and without which my time machine is powerless. But first things first. "I believe we can figure out how to refine your flying machine invention using cannon power, boosted through my solar panel, to find a way to create enough firepower to reverse the spiral and deliver me home."

"Yes, this is indeed possible." Leonardo stops, puzzled. "But first, explain to me how this flying machine might have the force—faster than one hundred horses harnessed to the flight of hawks, it would seem—"

"*Scusi,* Ser Leonardo. I fear that Maestro Lorenzo may indeed be searching for you and should he, in fact, enter and hear such talk—"

Bethy is acting all nervous, wringing her hands and pacing. As if Lorenzo's threats weren't enough to derail her life, seems she's got it bad for Lex. Crazy. Still, she saved my behind—I feel a newfound admiration for this unschooled girl, her intuitions, and her powers of persuasion.

"*Silencio, ragazza!*" Leo interrupts abruptly. "The prophetess Carlotta is on the verge of revealing knowledge that could transform Firenze, and perhaps the entire peninsula."

So I'm a prophet now? Not sure that's a good thing, under the circumstances.

"I'm only reporting the facts. But honestly, maestro, you have no idea. No idea! In the twentieth century, Albert Einstein proves that time and space are, in fact, one!"

"Unity of time and space. But this is heresy! Only God can see such things!" It's not clear whether this is what he really believes or if he's spouting off about God as a cover for any "listening ears." I am coming to appreciate that life in fifteenth-century Florence is a cross between spy drama and soap opera.

"You have proof of this?" Leonardo asks.

"Well, in fact . . ." I begin tapping harder on the tablet, thinking this reboot is scarily slow.

Bethy nervously interrupts. "Maestro Leonardo, you know the power of Fra Savonarola! If he were to learn of this witchery!"

"Bethy, will you just chill!" I exclaim. We learned mindfulness techniques in elementary school, and if there was ever a time to apply them, it's now!

"Savonarola barely needs any excuse to denounce you, Ser Leonardo. Your art alone he considers a challenge to God's grace that heralds the second fall of Man."

Wish I could teach Bethy to breathe, 'cause she is definitely losing her head.

"Savonarola cannot touch me, Elisabetta," Leonardo says. "I have powerful friends. And I will protect Carlotta's welfare as sure as the sun rises in the sky!"

"I'll take you up on that, maestro!" I say, hopeful that he can deliver on his word. "But meanwhile, space-time. Let me give you the Spark Notes version of Einstein's theory of relativity."

"Re-la-ti-vi-ty," Leo repeats reverently, with that sensual Italian rolling r.

"Um, so, let's see." I stop a moment, gathering my thoughts. If only I could get the tablet working again. No matter when and in what language you try to explain the theory of relativity, it's challenging. 'Cause if you haven't even gotten the basics of Galileo and Newton down yet . . .

"For starters, Maestro Leonardo, you yourself observed how sound moves in waves. Light also moves in waves. And particles. And Einstein showed how nothing can travel faster than light." I'm wondering if the math behind all this would be easier to understand. Of course, Leonardo applied geometry to his art.

"And space curves," I continue. "You have undoubtedly been aware of that in trying to capture three-dimensional landscapes as two-dimensional images in your paintings and sketches. I suggest this curvature of space through time is what will enable me to return to my time. Reversing the spiral."

I stop to see if he's getting this and—oh, how I wish Billy were here! Just to see how crazy it is that *I* am teaching the amazing polymath [my fave word ever: a person of great learning in several fields of study] Leonardo da Vinci.

But Leonardo has a puzzled look on his face.

"Oh, this is so hard to explain, Ser Leonardo!"

"Poor is the pupil—"

"No! You both must listen to me!" Bethy is not so interested in my lame attempts at explaining what must seem to her like Greek . . . or blasphemy; she keeps on sounding the alarm.

"*Calma, Elisabetta.*" Leonardo puts his hand up like a stop sign, overriding her alarm. "*Abbiamo cose più importanti da discutere.*"

More important matters indeed. There's nothing more important than my getting to Mamma.

I sigh. "So. Relativity. Here is what Einstein proved." I see, with some relief, a flicker of life in the old tablet. I made notes on the theory of relativity for the rocket camp I went to last summer—I think I can pull them up.

"Don't you understand?! The ears of the Inquisition are everywhere! Maestro, do you not see? Carlotta is not safe here!" Elisabetta is nothing if not insistent.

"Maybe if you look, Bethy, you will learn something," I reprimand her. Turning back to my tablet, I swipe through my notes, looking for a better explanation for the math behind Einstein's famous $E = mc^2$ formula.

"Here," I point, emphasizing the math formula on the screen. "We've learned the speed of light is constant."

"Constant," repeats Leonardo.

"*Si*, yes, light's speed is constant! Isn't that what I just said?" My frustration at not being able to explain five hundred–plus years of science at a glance is beginning to show. "And since we know that's true, according to Newton's laws—"

"Newton?" says Leonardo.

I smack my forehead. "Newton!" Of course, we're about two hundred years too early here. "I wish I had more time," I mutter. "But this is something of an international emergency. So you just must trust me here. . . ."

Something mysterious happens next: A video pops up—something I must've downloaded at camp and forgotten all about.

"Here's something," I sigh with relief, finding an easier explanation. "Einstein theorized that space and time are one and the same," I begin again, feeling my way.

Leonardo, who, I've learned, makes the abstract real by sketching everything he sees, pulls a scrap out of his folio and a charcoal from the pocket on his belt and starts sketching. I see the famous ringlets he uses to describe the swirling of air currents take shape—those that will one day be found in Ginevra de' Benci's hair.

"The function that the wing performs against the air when the air is motionless is the same as that of the air moved against the wings when these are without motion," Leonardo says.

"Wow, yeah, that's a pretty advanced aeronautics principle," I say. "We call it the Bernoulli effect because of the guy who discovered it. . . .

Er, given that we're here, and he's two centuries from now, maybe he really *re*discovered it."

But Leonardo's lost in his sketching. I peer over his shoulder. "But it's not so much about the curls, those currents you're drawing, as it is about the higher pressure of air beneath the wing, and lighter air as it flows over the top of the wing, say, of an airplane."

Leonardo looks up. *"Aria-piano? Questo?"*

"Here, look at this video!" I declare, seeing that the video is perfect for showing what I'm trying to explain and wondering if the universe is answering the question for me. I clap Translator to Leonardo's ears. He absently fits the purple muffs over his flowing hair. It's a pretty funny sight.

On screen, a pair of biplanes does loop the loops. "There's no single time for everybody in the universe. . . . ," intones the narrator, by way of explanation.

Leonardo raises an eyebrow while staring at the screen, trying to take it all in.

"... no distance in space that everyone can agree on," the voice continues as the antique (in my time) airplanes cross paths midair.

"*Aspetta!*" Wide-eyed, Bethy grabs for the tablet while saying something about silver birds that I can't quite make out.

"No, you wait! 'Cause that's exactly what I'm trying to explain!" I say, pulling the tablet away. "It's the Bernoulli principle that explains how airplanes fly." I wave my arms like wings. "Winged machines?"

"*Macchina volante?*" Bethy seems on the verge of freaking out again. Why do I even bother?!

"Bernoulli, *si.*" Leonardo is focused with laser-like intensity. "*Ancora!*" he commands when the video is done. When I hit play a second time, he signals I should pause it so he can study the airplanes' design.

"*Macchina volante,*" he whispers reverently. "*Volante, dico!*"

But now I realize this discussion is missing the point. This is not a lesson in aeronautics but about what we need to know to set the arrow of time to jump way forward, to my own century.

More to the point, though, I worry that if Leonardo da Vinci were to "discover" the theory of relativity hundreds of years before Einstein ...

Too late. Leo has torn Translator off his head and is excitedly sketching this new thing: the flying machine. The wing is exactly the glider design I saw on display at the Smithsonian's National Air and Space Museum—from here on out, I will know where Maestro Leonardo da Vinci downloaded the 411.

A Pandora's box, once opened, cannot be shut. But it's all in the name of science, isn't it? And besides, there's Mamma's predicament. I've gotta get back in time.

Leonardo grabs back my tablet and again touches the play button.

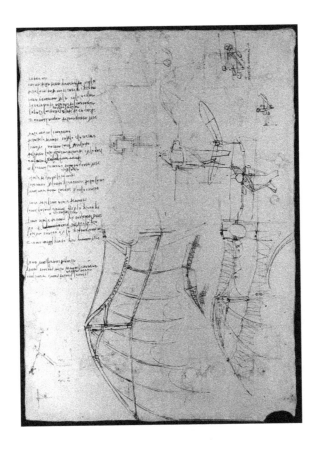

The barnstorming pilots once again throttle their biplanes skyward.

I look to see the maestro's reaction—he has dropped his hand, still clasping the screen, and gazes reverently up at the painted dome of sky in the vaulted ceiling above us.

"For once you have tasted flight, you will walk the earth with your eyes turned skywards, for there you have been and there you will long to return," Leonardo says reverently.

A breeze suddenly flows through the room, blowing Leo's folio to the floor. The torches lighting the room sputter and spurt with the wind. I feel a chill crawl up and down my spine. I swear, I can almost hear the whisper of the painted angels' flutterings.

Bethy scurries to pick up the pieces from Leonardo's papers as they skitter across the marble floors. She's muttering mysterious incantations: against ghosts, or the devil, I'm sure.

Leo has forced his gaze again at my tablet to inspect another video that's popped up in the queue; dreaming, no doubt, in the realm of the cosmos.

I feel my heart sinking. I've lost their attention. I can't explain how time is relative to one's movement through space. Or one twenty-first-century girl's need to beam back through space-time.

And, anyway, who am I to think I can outrun time? It was one thing to create the time machine with all the comforts and conveniences of modernity. It's quite another to do it without the science, tools, or technology.

Meanwhile, in real life, Savonarola's hunting me; we're about to add an unrecorded chapter to the history of science; Mamma's probably dying; and Dad—well, who knows how much trouble I've made for him. If only Billy were here right this minute to help me get Leonardo's attention back to matters at hand and help me puzzle out the problem!

But then I hear Dad's voice in my brain: "Focus, Charley. Don't give in to pity."

"Okay, Dad," I sigh. Which brings me back to the present. Er, past. I squeeze Translator over my ears and fluff out my hair, as per usual, to listen along with Leo.

"Let's try this again, maestro. About the unity of space and time . . ."

I hit the play button on yet another video: "Time Dilation," it's called. "Time stretches and contracts, varying with velocity. The faster you move through space, the slower you move through time."

I glance over to see if Leo's following along. "Time runs slower on Earth's surface, where you fall faster due to the magnification of gravity's effects by Earth's mass, than it does through space."

I see the cogs turning in Leonardo's brain as he takes this in. "So, then, time flows in relation to space in the same way your Bernoulli talks about air flowing to lift a flying machine? Earth is heavier than the atmosphere around it, thus time must move slower on Earth than in the heavens."

"Whoa, there you've got me, Ser Leo. I guess I never thought about it that way before," I confess, a bit stumped by his putting two and two together in this new way. "I mean, I'd have to check the math on that, and everything. . . ."

But he's too busy scrutinizing the wing he's sketched to hear my hesitation. I notice that when he's pleased with himself, he sports a self-satisfied little smile that I'd have to say closely mirrors the mysterious Mona Lisa smile that will one day be so iconic.

"Ahem. Anyways." I must stay focused. "Light speed, as I mentioned, is a whole other dimension, um, geometrically speaking. And that's what we need to achieve to get me home!"

The flames around us flicker again. In that twilight instant, this room is veiled in a smoky miasma. Bethy starts coughing. A smoke detector sure would make me feel better here.

"*Capisce?*" I ask him.

"*Si.* We need speed," he affirms, then repeats the explanation back in Italian; it's complicated to follow along, even with the earphones. I have to trust he's got it right.

But it's more than speed. "And, of course, it's not only atoms, but also the subatomic particles—invisible though they may be—that make up the material universe," I add for good measure. "It's like the cosmologists say: We all come from stardust."

Bethy looks away from the dome, staring down at her arms like she's never seen them before. "*Polvere di stelle?*" Even the ceiling angels seem to be frowning at this revelation. "You are saying that my body is made up of stars?"

"Well, yes, technically. The elements, like iron and calcium . . . oxygen, for sure. I guess you could look at it that way. . . ."

"But this is blasphemy!" Worry lines begin to dimple Elisabetta's otherwise unblemished face. She pulls up her voluminous skirts and fans the air around her legs as if expecting to see an oozing alien life-form instead of her own body.

It does kick up a lot of dust.

"*Polvere di stelle?!*" Bethy repeats, indignant. "You, perhaps, Carlotta. *Ma no, non me!*"

Not her, indeed.

"Not like that, Bethy," I try to reassure her. "It's not like a meteorite hit the planet and transformed, poof, into you! Although they do say that when Lorenzo de' Medici dies, a meteor lights the heavens over Firenze at his passing."

Given his earlier surprise that his patron would be dying later this year, I would've expected this news to get a rise from Leonardo. But Leo now seems deaf to the chatter around him.

I forge ahead. "But the atoms that make up our Earth, and our bodies, are the same as the atoms that make up the universe. The particles inside them are just configured differently and move at different speeds."

"This would seem to confirm," Leo pronounces, pacing, "that aspects of the material world can be converted into energy and vice versa, yes?" I guess he was paying attention after all. "Just as the snow in winter melts and turns into liquid water, and water moving in a river gathers force as it flows downstream . . . so the parts that make up other pieces of our world can, under the right conditions, transform into other states with a higher or lower flow of energy. Correct?"

Seeing the unseeable: that's the way Leonardo's mind works. Even skipping over half a millennium of scientific developments in physics, he can make the mental leap right to understanding that what seems solid and permanent can transform into another thing entirely, and that the other thing is what powers, well, everything. He seems to have intuited all this, like poets and artists through the ages.

"How did you get that so fast?"

"The painter has the universe in his mind and hands."

Here's someone who gets what it means to dream freely and create from your dreams. For one flash, I feel at home here.

Creating STEAM. In my day, they'll name that to show how science, technology, engineering, arts, and math combine.

I would call it genius. The minds of Leonardo, Newton, and Einstein, all brought together in one beautiful moment of creative momentum! While Einstein was not technically an artist (even though he did play the violin, like me!), he understood the power of the mind to dream. I have his quote up on my wall at home: "I am enough of the artist to draw freely on my imagination," he said. "For knowledge is limited to all we know and understand, while imagination embraces the entire world, and all there ever will be to know and understand."

It would take the imaginings of an Einstein, the speed of train travel, and rocket power technologies to prove what Leo has already imagined.

While I marvel, Leo's tone turns urgent. "For you then, *cara* Carlotta, that is the secret: transforming matter into energy. This is where we need to look."

"Bomb-diggity!" I exclaim, meaning not the actual nuclear one but a hooray for Leo's getting it so fast. As he jots notes in his folio, I get to inspect that famous right-to-left penmanship up close. As he's doing it, I practice mirror writing in the air with my finger. "Charley and Leo make time = emit ekam oeL dna yelrahC."

It's like a whole different language.

Leo's begun sketching the now-familiar "tepee frame"—to quote

Billy—the design that I originally saw and deduced to be the time machine, and that led me on this whole crazy experiment to begin with.

"It would seem one would have to animate a vast helix with enough energy," he observes as he sketches, "to speed up the interactions of atomic particles. . . ."

Wow, he's describing the kernel behind what would, in my day, become the CERN accelerator, in a massive laboratory that will be deep underground in a location not all that far from Tuscany, where scientists will one day define and measure previously undetectable quantum forces of the universe.

I am suddenly seized with a time traveler's shame. Did I let a dangerous genie out of its bottle? And will it be my fault if the future happens too soon?

As a girl of science, I know I share responsibility. But then again, wasn't it Leonardo himself who first saw the potential for pre-science . . . *prescience* . . . to upset the natural order (definition: science—knowledge of the things that are possible, present and past; prescience—knowledge of the things which may come to pass)?

"So, signorina. Let's determine what we need to create the forces that will get you back in time!"

Yes, let's, I think. "Elisabetta, do you know where my backpack is? *Scusi . . . dov'è la mia borsa?*" I ask her as sweetly as I can.

Apparently Bethy's still seeing stars. "How dare you interrupt God's order with your unnatural ideas!" she screams at me.

Well then! Despite my growing affection for her, it's clear Elisabetta cannot be dragged into a world so alien to her own (and here I think with irony of my dad's office and the "Welcome Aliens" sign on Take Your Child to Work Day).

I search around the sofa to see where she might have stowed my bag while I was hiding from Lorenzo. This takes a few minutes of my crawling around on my knees. And while the stardust idea might be controversial, the dust balls under the tables and chairs are in abundant evidence. Finally, I see a strap. I pull hard, panting from the exertion— it's hidden under a pile beneath a credenza—and liberate my backpack in a cloud. As the dust disperses, I sneeze again.

"*La strega Carlotta!* I will forevermore be cursed on account of you!"

"What, witch . . . me? Not at all. I am a girl of science." As I stand, I see Bethy has raised the tablet above her head and is poised to throw it to the ground, like a scene out of *The Ten Commandments,* that old movie they run on TV every year around Easter time.

"Don't you dare!" I quick grab it out of her hands before she can break it to smithereens, only to see the screen has gone dark again.

I stomp my feet in frustration. "Now you've done it, Bethy!"

She crosses her arms over her chest, unapologetic. "*Strega!*" she shouts back.

I'm about to read her the riot act when the tablet spontaneously reboots. The screen is still dark, but suddenly I hear a low conspiracy of voices. . . .

"I'm gonna rig a camera to my bike helmet so you can see where I am in case we get separated. You can see the feed on your phone."

"Billy?!" I cry out. I am so glad to hear his friendly voice again, if he were here I would kiss him. Another voice draws my attention back to the screen.

"Are you sure it's really a good idea to sneak into Mr. Morton's office, Billy?" It's Lex.

Bethy drops her hands to her sides and her eyes soften. She's heard it too!

"I mean, I've got a curfew, and my mom's gonna yell!" Lex insists.

"They are friends of yours, perhaps, Carlotta?" Leo asks, pulling the tablet close again and snatching Translator off my ears. "Eh, bene. Another vi-deo."

The screen is waking up again.

Bethy, perhaps forgetting that I'm the witch who's about to ruin her life, comes to stand next to me. As we listen, a familiar scene comes alive, like an Instagram video from home.

VI.
The Ultimate Weapon

Billy must have rigged up a head cam or something, 'cause I know he could never afford a GoPro. It's night, but I can tell in an instant the guys are outside in my home neighborhood!

I can see Lex take off on his bike. He's bundled up against the cold, and his backpack looks stuffed full. Billy's following close behind.

I feel a pit in my stomach.

"We're only doing what it takes to get Charley home, Lex. And since you were at least partly responsible . . ."

For the first time in ages, I breathe a sigh of relief.

"Dude! Whu'd I do? I can't help it if you brainiacs are out to rewrite history!" Lex is always acting blameless. "And you want to bring her back home? If it's true she's time traveled so far back, how do you know you'd even find her, much less get her to the right year?"

Billy ignores this. "C'mon, dude. I need your help. You gotta be there in case security shows up while I look around in the office where Charley said she got the code in the first place."

"How am I gonna do that, man? I don't know what to talk about to a stranger."

"Jeez, I dunno. Talk sports. That's something you're good at. And those night-watch guys are always watching sports on their monitors."

Bethy's eyes are practically popping out of her head as she stares at

Lex. *"Cosa stà dicendo, Carlotta?"*

I put up my hand to shush her. I'm afraid I'll miss something.

As I watch, the camera tilts up—Billy must be looking up—they're at Dad's office building! They ditch their bikes by dumpsters in back of the building, and Billy detaches the camera to switch it out with his Nats baseball cap. I watch as they pull orange coveralls that they must've found in the stash from Dad's workshop out of their backpacks and throw them over their street clothes.

I finally respond to Bethy. *"Ragazz pazzi.* They are absolutely nuts."

"Here, your, how you say—Translator, madonna?" Leonardo says, putting my purple muffs back over my ears. Guess he's heard about all he needs to know.

As for me, I can't take my eyes off the screen. Lex, from his demeanor, doesn't seem to be a hundred percent behind this stealth operation.

"I swear, Webhead," he announces quite loudly, "if anyone steals my wheels, it's *your* neck! My 'rents got me this for my fourteenth birthday, and it's, like, top o' the line, man."

"Shut up, idiot!" Billy hisses. "Big yikes if someone hears us! We gotta see if there's a way to sneak in; bet the night cleaning crew comes out at some point and props the door open long enough to throw garbage in the dumpster."

Elisabetta catches the word *idiot* and frowns. *"Lex non è un'idiota!"* she shouts at Billy. *"Lui è bello!"*

"He can't hear you, Bethy," I observe. "But you're half-right—girls at home call him 'Sexy Lexy.'"

"Sex-y, Lex-y," she apes back. *"Questo sex-y?"*

"Some say that Michelangelo's sculpture of David portrays one of the sexiest men on earth," I attempt by way of explanation.

"Buonarroti?" Leonardo breaks in. "The stonecutter's apprentice has carved no David!"

Oops. My bad. Michelangelo's *David*: another not yet.

"Well, sexy is . . ." I think for a minute, then make a kissy face and smooch the air, cracking Bethy up. She then gives a more credible show of sexiness from bottom to top, swooshing her skirts, sliding her blouse off her shoulders, and finishing off with a toss of her hair and a slow blink.

"*Affascinante*," Leonardo corrects.

As he enunciates the universal take on sexy, I am sure I am blushing.

A clatter emanating from the tablet calls my attention back. Billy, klutzier even than me, has seemingly toppled the first in a line of metal bins, causing a domino effect.

"Oh, man! Wouldn't they have a ton of security cameras back here, Billy?"

But Billy, hoisting the first metal bin back up, isn't paying attention. Instead, he seems to be trying to determine his next best move before anybody responds to the clatter. I see him making a dash for the door by the loading dock. It swings open. Someone must've left it ajar.

"*Psst*, Lex! C'mere. I think we found a way in!"

"Sexy!" Bethy says admiringly. "Oh, why does time separate me from my new true love!"

Her love. Here we go again! This Bethy's gonna be lovin' and leavin' 'em across the ages.

Leo, having gone back to sketching, looks from his notes to me and back again. He stands and comes over toward me and, with his hands and eye, seems to measure me for height and weight.

"At last, I understand. A weapon that might be useful for something beyond war."

I sneak a look at his designs: a bicycle. Plus a cannon. Plus me—equals bike-powered human cannonball!

"Umm—not sure I can be your human guinea pig, Ser Leonardo." I mean, after being the near miss of his midnight multi-barreled cannon-firing experiments, no *grazie*!

He's thinking of me as a human matter-to-energy experiment. A wind again blows through the room, sending chills up my spine. Leonardo, who had been oblivious to these gusts until now, this time takes notice.

"Ah, but they are setting up for Carnevale. Their masked ball," Leonardo informs us. "The troubadours and entertainers must be arriving. And no doubt the kitchen will be preparing for the evening's elaborate feast."

He would know—if I know my Leonardo history, he's been busy staging all these elaborate court entertainments for the duke of Milan.

"I suspect they've opened all the doors to set up for the festivities."

Bethy again looks spooked. "No! There are phantoms in this *sala*. I feel them! See here!" She lays her fingers on the tablet as if it's a Ouija board that will reveal the identities of whatever so-called spirits may be in the room.

I take off Translator—if there's something going on in the room besides us three talking, I need to be able to hear. I check out the tablet screen again, and what it is showing is like nothing I've ever seen. "What in the world?!"

As we watch, Billy's latest move in TeenWords pops up under Bethy's fingers and begins shifting and scrambling letters. They appear, marching out in a row, then transform into others. And then, when the app stops this frantic dance, random letters completely disappear!

I stare, mystified. It appears this is no usual game of TeenWords! This game's gone haywire—or else Billy's reprogrammed it. And why would he do that?

There's gotta be a clue here: I have to make sense of it. My eyes focus in on the screen, trying to solve the scramble: three Es, a T, two Ns, one M . . . "ET phone home!" I call out wildly, jumping up and down. As if anyone would get that reference! "Et tu, Brute!" That couldn't be it, no Ns or Ms. "Give me an S!" I shout, feeling like a contestant on *Wheel of Fortune*.

Elisabetta, awakened from her spell by my antics no doubt, mimics my gestures, laughing and shouting.

A tap on the shoulder breaks my concentration. I turn, but no one's there. Elisabetta's ghosts?

Then, a tap on the other.

"*Carlotta, ho un mesaggio per te!*"

I turn again, ready to yell at the rude interrupter, even if it's Lorenzo the Magnificent himself.

"*Carlotta—prego!*"

I turn to see two imploring brown eyes looking over my shoulder. "Carolina!"

"*Si, prego, Tcharr-li. È Savonarola . . . ha sentito di una strana ragazza con una pietra magica che prevede il futuro. Lui manda i Piagnoni a Firenze per cercare di fermarla.*"

With her shotgun delivery, I have no idea what she's talking about, but Carolina's sudden appearance and the panic in her voice makes me forget all about solving the puzzle.

"*Come fa a saperlo, il Fra Savonarola?*" Leonardo asks, butting in between me and Carolina.

What does Savonarola know, indeed!

Her brown eyes grow wider. "*Le scarpe, Ser Leonardo. I ragazzi!*" The boys. "*Essi portarono le scarpe a Fra Savonarola. Della magia.*" Magic?

She's pointing to my booted feet while stomping her own. *Scarpe* are . . . boots? I look from Carolina to Leonardo and back again. Did Signora Vincenzo steal these boots for me? I puzzle over the few words I could pick out. Boys . . . boots . . . magic. I don't get it!

Seeing my confusion, Leo refits Translator over my ears.

"Those boys! They say you possess magic!" Bethy II exclaims. "I chased those crazy boys away—me and Vil-burrrr."

"*Pazzi*, perhaps. Like foxes." Carolina is hopping around like a Mexican jumping bean. She jumps to where Bethy is standing. "And even so, Elisabetta, you are not safe! They say you are also *una strega*, like *Tcharr-li!*"

"My shoes!" I cry, piecing her words together. "Those boys at the river stole my shoes!"

Leo interjects, "It seems they not only stole them, but brought them to Savonarola as evidence to be used against you."

"What?! My stupid ballet flats as evidence? Of what not to wear for time travel?"

"Oh, they are merely angry that I wouldn't kiss them!" pouts Bethy, the Ultimate Flirt. "Or . . . perhaps they wanted Vil-burrr back?"

Leo has been pacing all this time, so lost in thought I doubt he was even listening. "We have not a moment to lose then."

Elisabetta snaps to attention. *"Dio* me! I promised *Magnifico* I would send for the carpenter and a painter. The painting—" She points to the masterpiece, precariously propped up against the sofa, which I now recognize as Botticelli's *Primavera*. It is a little, well, *Affascinante*.

"Wait . . . I know this work! Is that what he was yelling about when I was stumbling back there in the dark?" I point to the wall.

She nods. "I must fetch a craftsman to repair the walls, retouch the gilding, and reaffix this painting." She steps up and looks at the subject, as if seeing *Primavera* for the first time. "Why *Magnifico* cares so about mere strokes of paint on canvas is a mystery, anyway—especially when he can order Botticelli to paint another!"

Leonardo tut-tuts, as if dismissing this famous masterpiece and its painter.

I can't help thinking there's a lot more to it. "There is no time, Bethy! Savonarola—"

She waves her hand dismissively. "Savonarola is not such a danger, but my mamma, she is another story. I am to help prepare the heaps of food ordered for tonight's masked ball. If I fail to deliver—there goes our livelihood, and my hide with it!"

She stops and, for a moment, straightens tall, flashing a proud smile. "La Taverna Vincenzo has been invited to contribute our specialty for *Magnifico's* esteemed guests tonight—stuffed roast piglet in vinegar!"

"Wilbur!" I shout, clapping my hand over my mouth in horror.

But Bethy's laughing! "Why, yes, of course. I warned you, Carlotta! How else could I satisfy *Magnifico* and Mamma at one and the same time?" Her smile fades.

Carolina's hand shoots to the sky. "*A me! I* can run for help, Elisabetta! Do not worry! *Ecco Carolina, al tuo servizio!*"

The little sprite dashes away in a flash.

Meanwhile, Leonardo is scrutinizing Billy's TeenWords upgrade—the morphing word scramble. "Carlotta, this equation: EINSTEIN E = mc²."

Hurrying to look over his shoulder, I see the letters have resolved themselves into the famous formula. And then some kind of embedded video pops up and the formula morphs onto a grid showing Earth warping and twisting, the action of bodies moving through the space-time continuum described by Einstein's equation.

Well then! No need to buy a vowel: Leo's solved the puzzle. In the back of my mind, I wonder if Kairos isn't involved. This is the same spinning Earth that appeared when he hacked into the ultra-secure servers at Dad's office—he's here, he's there, he's everywhere. Shouldn't surprise anybody at this point that Kairos has powers greater than any I know of, even five centuries from now. Makes me wonder what century he actually hails from—this one, mine, or one yet to come? And then there's the mystery of why he would pick *me* to reveal his secrets.

Can't worry about it. I stamp my feet to ground myself, 'cause back

here on planet Renaissance, I have other matters to attend to, namely, the quantum-qualia education of Leonardo da Vinci.

"Our planet. Earth. And Albert Einstein. Like you heard, he proved—"

Bethy, staring over my shoulder, interrupts. "Tell me," she insists, "what do the letters say? Earth—she is a ball?"

"*Sì.* Well, not precisely round as a ball," I reply. "But the Earth is a globe."

This girl is all over the place. One minute, she's scared of phantoms, and before you can say "boo," she's fixated on the animated Earth-ball turning in space.

She pulls the tablet away again to examine Einstein's formula, pulling it up close and shutting first one eye then the other, then holding it out at arm's length and squinting. "*No capisce,*" she murmurs.

Still, she has the curiosity and the drive to know. That's the most important thing when it comes to learning, even as Leo has shown us.

It occurs to me that Bethy might need glasses if ever we were to do a reading lesson.

"And your Maestro *Eye-n-stey-n*—he lives on the Earth?"

"Well, not exactly. You see, he died a long time ago and—" I stop, realizing that time, being relative, has no meaning here.

"What do these letters say?"

"E equals M times C squared," I recite. "Energy equals mass times the speed—"

"This goes beyond perfect geometry," Leo is muttering. "Unlike the Fibonacci sequence, whose elegance pertains only to the material world."

Bethy's oblivious to the maestro's mental meanderings. I can see she's trying to figure out what the whole Earth-on-grid image has to do with her. "And Earth—she will fall into this vortex—this is God's prophecy?"

"Well, you see, there's this whole other thing I was just explaining to Ser Leonardo about gravity, and . . ." I can see this is going way over her head. "Never mind. Give me the tablet, Bethy. It's not even mine, really. It belongs to *mio padre*, and he likely will kill me for hacking into it! That is, if I ever see him again." My eyes blur with tears, but I must keep the physics lesson going if I am ever going to get Leo to focus on a solution with me.

Leo's eyes are scanning the screen intently. "Airwaves. These, I have tried to depict in my sketches. I have speculated, of course. Your Alberto *Eye-n-stey-n* is brilliant to have proved this mathematically. Of course, he and your Ser Isaac Newton improved vastly on my poor powers of observation. *Re-la-tiv-i-ty.*"

He stops marveling and looks up with a glint in his eye. "*Capische! Dum loquimur, fugerit invida aetas, carpe diem, quam minimum credula postero!* I'll begin preparations at once. Carlotta, I will need your assistance to perfect this plan."

Translator spits out a rush of what sounds like Latin. Must be a glitch. I recognize that *"carpe diem"* from first-year Latin: "seize the day"—or "pluck" it, as my Latin teacher—a stickler for accuracy—insists. Wish I could look up the rest of the quote.

Leonardo looks well pleased. *"Incredibile!* What a gift you have given me, Carlotta. You, Elisabetta! You will keep a hawk's-eye watch on our brainy visitor."

"Ser Leonardo, *mia madre* will be so angry. . . ."

"She will have to wait." Leonardo looks annoyed. "I must go to my atelier to sketch out the plans. Too many distractions here in the palace."

"Then where shall I go, what with the danger here, Leo?"

Carolina shyly takes my hand. "You will be safe in the secret passage here, *Tcharr-li.*" She leads me to the fake panel in the wall behind where *Primavera* was hung. "It is for the best that you remain hidden for now."

"Yes, Carlotta. It's best if you remain hidden. Quiet as the grave," Leonardo warns ominously. "And you, Carolina, must divert Fra Savonarola."

"But, Ser Leonardo!" Bethy interrupts again. "What shall I tell *Magnifico* if he should look to find you?"

"Tell him I am working on the ultimate weapon," he responds. Gathering up his drawings, he takes one quick peek at my tablet again. "*E miracolo!*" he exclaims, shaking his head as he strides from the room.

VII.
TIME WARP

Thanks to my enforced incarceration, and my panicky prison warden, Elisabetta, I have a spare moment to update the blog. TeenWords is too tedious to get across all that's happened. Besides, the letters I need don't always come up. Or, in Billy's latest version, they'd probably scramble uncontrollably. Runaway words.

Blog Entry #6. Still FYEO.

I know where you are—and it worries me. You guys could get in BIG trouble! I'm deeply grateful you would go that far to help me . . . but really, like, what the heck is your plan?!

Getting Leo up to speed here. Each time we make some progress with our lesson on the physics of time travel, he finds some reason to disappear. More than a little frustrating!

Billy, while I'm here, I'm gonna soak up as much as I can. I suspect Kairos is privy to more than Top Secret stuff: He's everywhere at once. He even made contact with Mamma in Florence-future. Yes, really. In fact, I am a tiny bit disappointed that he seems to be more in the know than Leonardo himself—although, don't be fooled! Leo is every bit the superhero that history holds him out to be!

Then there's Bethy II. I had my doubts—she's as boy crazy as our Beth, but she has an instinctive intelligence—some deeply compassionate ambition at work in that girl.

You know I'm usually not one to complain. But except for accidentally swallowing some water at the horse trough, I haven't eaten anything but a few gummy worms and an energy bar in, like, 500 years! And I have no intention of sticking around long enough for Columbus to bring back the tomato.

Which brings me to my point, Billy. While being here is truly a once-in-a-lifetime, and Leo's giving me some amazing quotes for our report, I need to get back. Like, I'm guessing you're trying, given the office break-in and all, but I cannot stress enough the seriousness of all this. So give me a clue on how we can come up with a plausible plan to GET ME BACK HOME!!!! And I mean pronto, Billy!

'Cause there's a dark side to all this Renaissance light: the preacher, Savonarola.

Savonarola seems to have gotten word that I can see the future, and this tablet only adds fuel, so to speak, to that particular bonfire! "Una strega"—a witch—Leo informs me, is how they'd justify applying the torch. Youch!!!

So far, no one knows what I know except Leo and, to the extent she has seen your face and Lexy's, Bethy II. And probs il Magnifico suspects something. And Carolina, Signora Vincenzo, Viola . . . whoa.

Then, there's Mamma: Something's not right with her. I need to get to her! So, true confessions here: I'm scared. Help!

Your PITT, Charley

P.S. If you do manage to materialize anything back here,
could you try to send me a can of Pringles or something? Here,
they're all like, "Let them eat pig!"

I'm not sure how much time has passed when the tapers in my hiding place flicker, and I am reminded that I'd be dumb to stick around watching the screen all day.

I shut the tablet decisively, praying I'll get another chance to spy on the guys at home at some point.

I knock on the wall. "Olly, olly oxen free!" I whisper, hoping against hope for the all clear.

The panel gives way with a creak. Ignoring Leonardo's dictum to watch that I don't go anywhere, Bethy grabs me by the arm and starts to pull.

"*Viene con me,* Carlotta! I must run to *devo correre a casa* to help *la mia mamma.*"

I nod and let Elisabetta drag me. As we make our way out into the street again, I notice a growing number of citizens milling around—people of all ages, sizes, and shapes—many carrying masks and noise-makers. Children run with streamers and banners, singing and shouting; it's like New Year's Eve in Times Square, only with Lorenzo's guardsmen on horseback to keep the peace instead of New York's Finest. Carolina must be somewhere in here. And we're in the midst.

But Bethy's weaving in and out, not paying attention to the crowd.

"Hey, Elisabetta, wait up!" I call, but she can't hear me over the din. I notice that my foot is not hurting as much as it did before—so I think I can pace her.

She looks back over her shoulder, frowning. "If I don't get home in time, Mamma will have my neck!"

I am not as worried about Bethy's personal family drama as I am that one of Savonarola's peeps may be searching for us.

"Bethy! Don't you think we should hide ourselves a little?"

She comes to a dead stop. "Hide? *No, perché?*" she asks innocently.

"Spies!" I hiss. "You don't think Savonarola . . . ?"

"Oh, why do you keep on about that priest so, Carlotta? Do not fear," she insists. "*Mi mamma e Viola*—they are *Piagnoni*. They will warn us!"

What is she talking about, *Piagnoni*? Rings a bell, but . . . why? Time for a mental scan—*Piagnoni, Piagnoni, Piagnoni*—this word does not compute. Not even with the powers of Translator. If our game hasn't been messed up forever, must try that out on Billy in TeenWords—if I ever get another chance!

Meanwhile, I feel my phone vibrating. Didn't realize it was on mute 'cause, frankly, who could be calling me here?!

But irony has no place in a world that doesn't follow any of the normal rules. "Whoa, Bethy!" I grab her arm and pull her aside with a warning look. We duck into a dark alley. The screen on my phone is dimming and I wonder if I can find enough light this late in the day—and a place to rest long enough—to deploy the solar battery for a recharge.

But it's not a phone call. The screen has mysteriously come to life just like my tablet: Billy and Lex. It looks as if they were able to sneak into Dad's office, because I recognize the anteroom where Kairos was hanging out during TYCTW Day. To my surprise, there's even what looks like a copy of Kairos's maquette—the one I first saw in Dad's office that somehow held the key to my launching back half a millennium— on the desk.

"Weird," I say out loud.

"*Qual'è il mistero?*" Elisabetta repeats back in a question.

"The *modello*, Horse and Rider," I say, pointing to the screen. I thought I had it with me. Since we are well hidden, I set down my backpack to ferret through the junk inside. "It's not here!"

"*Un bel modello!*" she notes, not getting that the thing was *here* and now it's *there.*

But I can't waste time on that now. Back in my dad's office, I see Billy checking out papers on the desk.

"We need clues, Lex," he says in a loud enough whisper for the immediate world to hear. I see Lex standing by the office door, keeping watch. "Like this . . ."

"What, Webhead—whatdya find?" Lex asks, still peering out into the hallway.

"This manual," Billy says. "Mentions something about Operation Firenze. So that's a real thing!"

I can see what Billy's looking at now—it's got a big warning written in red across the cover. "TERCES POT." I recognize this language—and the handwriting, for that matter. TOP SECRET. Word-mashups in mirror writing. Leonardo's way of protecting his trade secrets.

"Wait, man. Lemme get a look," Lex says, hurrying over. I can see that he's got his phone out and is busy snapping pictures.

"You guys!" I yell. "Secret means SECRET. You should NOT be taking pictures in there." Hopeless. They cannot hear me.

But truth be told, I'm for whatever it takes to get me home.

Lex says, "Got the picture-taking wrapped up. Hey, Billy, where ya goin'?"

Billy has moved out of the anteroom. "This must be Mr. Morton's office," he murmurs, and because I know Billy so well, I detect excitement in his voice. From what I can see on my phone, he's in front of my dad's computer. The same one that Kairos hijacked remotely way back when, before I entered the vortex or knew it even existed.

"Whoa—I can't believe—come look at this, Lex!"

"Wait a sec, I've gotta grab one more shot. . . ."

"Holy spirits . . . ," I begin. Because the visual I'm getting on Dad's computer is looking eerily familiar.

"*Sanctu spiritu* . . . ," Bethy echoes. Because what she's looking at is the beautiful Lex.

No matter. The Google Earth view on Dad's monitor looks like the same program Kairos planted there before, and the one that showed up in TeenWords, looping over and over.

No. Could Kairos know that Billy . . . and I. But no, that's impossible.

"Awesome, man." Billy's touching the screen reverently as if trying to soak up the numbers and equations through his fingers. They are morphing, seemingly on their own, into shapes. First circles, cylinders, cyclones, and the like. Then shapes that I've never seen before—ones that have only been predicted on the quantum scale.

"It's . . . it's . . . you know, like, a visualization of the time-space warp. Multiple dimensions beyond the four we know, folded in on each other. Magnified." Billy stumbles over his words, even as he finds a scrap of paper and, as numbers pop up suddenly, begins jotting down equations that somehow seem to match their geometric equivalent on the screen.

Now, despite my predilection for scientific discovery, math has never been my strongest suit, which is why I have worked extra hard at it. As for the wonder of numbers, that's what I have Billy for. So whatever magic he's seeing in these scrambling and unwinding digits, I'm gonna have to take his word for it.

"Hey, Webhead," Lex interjects suddenly. "Check this out!"

The numbers fade out as these weird geometrical shapes appear to self-animate. They quickly morph into anime figures, flashing in hyperspeed, running, spinning, and aflame, as if engaged in battle, arrows arcing in trajectories forward to various points in time from 1492. Every time a character disappears, the scene reshuffles forward in time.

"This. Is. So. Awesome." Billy breathes. "Someone is putting history on a mad timeline. Seems there could be peeps besides me and Charley working on time travel."

Lex watches for a moment, absorbed in what's on the screen. "Either that, or someone has created the coolest video game ever!" Lex exhales. "Better than Minecraft even. Wonder where the controls are?"

After a minute or so, I can hear what sounds like Lex's fingers tapping on the desk, like he's pretending to pound on a controller. He takes a deep breath in.

Billy glances over at Lex, and I can see he's got that slack-jawed fish face boys get when their brains have been taken over by the digital gods of gaming. Obviously enraptured with the scene unfolding on the screen, he would appear blissfully ignorant of anything outside the game.

But I'm not. I can hear footsteps outside the purview of the video feed, and the creak of something like a cleaning cart.

"Um, you guys . . . ?" Somehow, I'm getting that we've got only one-way audio. Wish they could hear me like I can hear them.

"What is Lexy saying, Carlotta?" Bethy asks. I almost forgot she was here. "Will he be in danger? I am so worried about—"

"Shh!" I hush her. I have to get a warning to them. The footsteps seem to be growing louder at Dad's, and I hear a woman's voice over the jangle of keys.

"Who the hell left all the lights on here!" an insistent female voice complains off camera. "And why didn't the cleaners secure the offices on this hall!"

"Did you hear somebody, Billy?" Lex asks, tearing his eyes away from the screen. Thank goodness he's returned from game-land.

"Hey, you. Billy!"

Billy finally looks up and scans the room too. "Dunno. Whatdya hear, Lex?"

"Dunno. A . . . somebody. Sounded mad."

Yes, Lex, you're right! I'm hoping, if I concentrate hard enough, they'll catch my warning telepathically.

It's quiet on their end a minute before Lex whispers, "Um, Billy? Do you think we'd better, um . . . maybe, like, go?"

The woman speaks up again, louder. "Don't they know about all the secret business going on in these offices? And now, what with all the planted trolls and bots hacking classified programs!"

Lex looks in Billy's direction. I can see he's like a deer caught in headlights.

The voice is sputtering now in grievous protest. "How am I supposed to do my job on night watch if all I'm doing is other people's jobs!" She must be right on them. I hold my breath.

"LEXY! *BEE-LY!* DO SOMETHING!" This time it's Bethy mobilizing them. "RUN! There are spies!"

Beneath my very eyes on the screen, it seems like Lex must've heard her. 'Cause next thing, he's uncharacteristically taking charge of things.

"Dive, Billy! Under the desk—no, wait." Lex touches a button, and as Bethy and I stare, a wall opens partway in front of them to reveal an A/V-like control room, with what looks to be projection equipment and a digital library. It's kind of like the secret panel in Lorenzo's palazzo— only way more high-tech. "Billy, c'mere. Quick. I found a better place."

"Hold on a sec, Lex." Billy pulls out a flash drive and copies something from Dad's computer. "If I can find the source code for this crazy program . . ."

He clips the flash drive to a loop inside his backpack along with a few additional papers and supplies lying loose on the desk, including the Operation Firenze manual.

"Hey, no kiddin'. I'm outta here, man," Lex says, disappearing behind the wall.

I see Billy shoving more stuff into his backpack. Looks like he's wrapping up the maquette and packing that too. He takes a backward glance; everything still looks in order. When who should show up silhouetted in the computer-lit anteroom?

Kairos!

Billy freezes. "Who's there?" I hear Billy ask under his breath, as he looks around.

I want Billy to make a run for safety, but I'm also trying to get a closer look at Kairos. He's such a dead ringer for the man in the sculpture, he must've been the model, unless, that is, Kairos has a twin brother. In Kairos's hands is a beautiful instrument that now emits a sweet, familiar sound.

"My violin!" I cry out at strains of a familiar tune being plucked from its strings. "But who told him he could play it?"

Even mad as this should make me, I can't resist humming along. Suddenly, I'm itching to draw a bow across its strings, to evoke the sonorous notes of the sound poem me and Mamma wrote.

Bethy's turn to shush me. "Why do you sing so loud, Carlotta! Do you want them to find us here!?" She creeps up to the front of the alleyway and peeks into the piazza to make sure I haven't given us away.

But I can't help humming and swaying to my song. For one brief instant, I allow myself to be lost in the music. The violin pulls me into a space and time where I am a girl who is able to abide across time. With that, the craziness and panic of this moment fades.

I am free.

Hearing my old instrument—this close and yet impossibly far—hope and sadness overwhelm me. It seems unimaginable to be able to be where one wants at precisely the moment one wants to! Isn't that relativity in its most conscious form?

I envy Kairos's mastery. Why not me? Why can't I: 1). Learn

Leonardo's secret to not let anyone get in the way of your passions; 2). Present the winning project for the Da Vinci Middle School Science Fair; and 3). Be with my mamma, to play our song and help her get well?

Maybe this is my own apprenticeship.

"Elisabetta, do you hear?" I demand, walking closer to her lookout. "There they were—Billy and Lex—he ran when you said. . . . But then, big surprise—there's Kairos! In the anteroom. I am not kidding—that kid's everywhere at once. Like, what's the deal with that?"

But Bethy, suddenly all innocence, stares at the ground, tracing her toe round and round in the dirt. As she lifts her foot I see the shape she

has left imprinted on the ground: a whirlwind.

"It is all as you have said, Carlotta!" she intones mysteriously. "Music transforms the world. You are an alchemist of highest order!"

And in that moment, the sweet strains of violin music that have been seeping out from the phone and pouring into my heart grow louder. Backing farther away from the street to avoid detection, I fix my eyes on that other scene: As Kairos plays, Billy is tiptoeing up to the new wall opening where Lex disappeared. And as I'm watching—from the outside this time—the same vortex of energy, colors, and images that swirled around and pulled me here envelop Billy.

A strong gust suddenly blows through the alleyway where we're standing, creating a wind tunnel, very loud, sweeping away the strains from my violin. And it's kicking up a lot of dust. I start coughing again, and as I wipe my eyes on my sleeve, I happen to look down at the whirls that Bethy has traced. They've blown up in the wind to form now-eddying dust devils.

"What is happening, Carlotta?" Bethy yells against the wind. Her hair is blowing wildly and I wonder what my own mop must look like. Mamma would be so upset with me!

"It's Billy! He's caught in the vortex!" I holler back above the wind. In fact, the energy we're experiencing feels like an echo of the airwaves I rode to get here, to the same earth-shaking, ear-shattering effect. Why wouldn't it take me home again?

All of which has me wondering what could've kicked up the vortex, first in our garage, then in Dad's office. I mean, a dust devil out of doors may be semi-explainable, but in a temperature-controlled high-rise building where the windows don't even open to the outside?

I wonder if anyone else is experiencing this parallel reality—or if Billy's virtual worlds aren't really more rational than the one we're living in. Kairos, still fiddling, slows the tempo from allegro to lento, and finally brings the music to a close. Though I can barely hear it under the wind. The cyclone that was stirred up in two time zones dies.

But.

Billy is gone.

Let me say for the record: Everyone knows I am a girl of science. With enough advances in research, I know the supernatural can be explained. I do not believe in magic, much less music's power to harness the energies of the universe. But Billy was there and now he's not. How to account for this—and the space-time breach that brought me here? Who is Kairos and how to fit into any knowable context the knowledge that he materializes across time and space, seemingly at will?

Idk. I don't know. I *am aching* to know. Soon. And I need to know where in the universe Billy disappeared to . . . though based on experience, I do have an inkling. The idea that he is totally lost is no longer top-of-mind for me; from my own experience, I am betting he'll show up eventually.

And though it's plausible that the whirlwinds we experienced could disrupt our communications, I am still seeing scenes of Dad's office.

I continue to stare for what seems an eternity at the static screen until I realize waiting will have a cost. Bethy has abandoned her lookout to brush the dust from her dress and arms. I don't mention that her face is dotted with dirt. "Maybe we should hightail it back to your mamma's?"

"*Un momento, Carlotta!*" she insists, pointing at the phone screen. "There is someone. I feel it. *Dove* Lexy?"

"Coward!" I spit, suddenly mad at him. Lex could've totally saved Billy from whatever that was.

"No. *Attenzione!*" she hisses.

She's right, of course, to keep paying attention—here and there, both. It's late afternoon and it's beginning to grow dark. The temperature must be dropping as the sun goes down, 'cause I feel a shiver down my back. And though there is no one at the moment nearby, that doesn't mean we are safe.

"Bethy, yell if you see someone entering the alley."

A subtle sound draws my eyes back to the screen. Outside the anteroom to my father's office, I catch a glimpse of a security officer in uniform, a no-nonsense middle-aged woman, short but solid. It's dark, so I can't see her face, but by the purpose in her step, I'm pretty sure she heard whatever sound came from my violin and the explosion that followed.

This night watchwoman—if that's who she is—is about to enter Dad's office, and no doubt, she could sniff out Lexy if he's still hiding back there. She holsters her walkie-talkie and pulls out a flashlight, sweeping the room several times over.

"Someone is searching!" Bethy yells, a little too loudly.

"Huh?" I jump, startled. Apparently Bethy has a hard time following directions because she's still staring over my shoulder, pointing at what's happening on the screen.

"Hmm. Things are not quite right here." The watch lady is talking to herself. "Is there a little mouse in hiding? Come out, little mouse!"

She walks into Dad's office and, from the doorway, shines the light deeper into corners and beneath the table covered with files. Nothing seems out of place to my eye, and apparently not to hers either. She pulls off the large key ring that is clipped to her belt as if ready to lock the office against intruders.

But then she jerks her head around and drops the keys, which clatter against the ancient linoleum floor.

"Oh!" Bethy moves in closer, squinting at my screen. Spectacles are definitely in order. "Viola?"

"Viola who?" I ask, wondering how in the world Bethy would

recognize anyone in Dad's office.

"*Mia cugina. Esta mia cugina!*"

"Your cousin? What are you talking about?" I ask, annoyed that I can't at least get a sense of Lex's whereabouts from here.

"*Si.* That is Viola." Bethy's eyes grow wide.

"Viola. Impossible!" I exclaim.

"I think I would know my own cousin!" she replies huffily. "Where in the world . . . ?"

I peer closer at the screen, wishing the lights were on in Dad's office, and wondering whether I should pull out my tablet to stretch the image. But there is something about the body type . . . and the way she carries herself. Still, even if my being here proves that time travel is possible, nothing larger than a quantum particle can be in two places at once.

"You're crazy, Bethy! They may look alike, but—"

"*Eh, no!*" she interrupts my logical brain with a news flash. "She is moving near Lexy!"

And I see that Viola—or whoever she is—is about to open the closet that is probably Lex's current hiding place. Wish I could warn him, until I see Bethy applying her apparently deep powers of concentration in what might be actual evidence of mental telepathy across time.

Viola flips a switch, and a narrow control room of sorts appears. It's loaded with all the electronics, screens, and bells and whistles of a video production studio. Geez, if I had only known that Dad's office was adjacent to such a cool maker space when I visited!

And then the scene switches, as if a video producer has called for a camera change in a live TV production. The ancient Greeks would call this a deus ex machina moment: god dropping in from out of the machine to save the day. Amazingly, I see a tensely frozen Lex sitting on the floor, his back wedged against the door, ear pushed up to the wall. He's gripping my violin by the neck. *Don't break the strings, don't break the strings, don't break the strings,* I pray. Not sure whether he saw Billy's fireworks departure, but I imagine that such a visual might feel traumatic; Lex has seen two friends vanish into thin air in the past twenty-four hours.

"*It wasn't the kiss. It wasn't the kiss,*" he whispers over and over.

Bethy starts pounding on my shoulder, begging to know what he said. "Will he be okay?"

I am about to say that I cannot see into the future, but instead I give a grim laugh; that whole "lack of foresight" thing wouldn't exactly be true for me anymore, would it?

The scene switches back to Viola, who is shining her flashlight around the control room. I freeze when I see her shine a light on a video monitor that seems to be running the same video game Lex marveled at earlier with Billy, except it is spelling out a message—and it looks to be in mirror writing:

".emoh gninruter ni attolraC tsissa ot alumrof laropmet eht em dneS .soriaK aiv icniV ad .L atsE"

To the best of my ability, I scan that right to left: "Esta L. da Vinci via Kairos. Send me the temporal formula to assist Carlotta in returning home."

Whoa. So Kairos is the mastermind—or at least Leo's agent. It would appear he's feeding back info on my homies to Leonardo, who's asking them to help him with some big data. And I mean BIG.

This is way too much for my pounding head to ponder.

Bethy again grabs the phone from my hand to squint at the screen, then puts it to her ear. "*Qualcosa non và!*"

No duh, something's wrong! As a quick recap: I'm stuck; Billy's vanished; Lex is about to be discovered by this other Viola, who looks suspiciously like Bethy II's cousin; Leo's writing in a code designed to be deciphered in my century; Mamma is probably dying; Bethy and I are about to be tried for witchcraft . . . and the punishment if we're found guilty? BURNING AT THE STAKE. What could possibly be right with this picture?

But then I notice what Bethy's fussing over on the screen—something rustling out of the shadows . . . and hello, Kairos! He's walking slowly toward the bank of monitors near the closet where Lex is hiding out. So that's why we've remained tuned in—Kairos is there reporting live.

He's concealing something in his left hand, and even in the dimly lit control room I can see it glinting. He slowly stretches out his right hand, apparently to adjust something on the screen, and loses his balance, letting go of the glinty thingy, which clatters to the tile floor.

"The golden compass!" I gasp.

"Aha! I knew it." Viola, or whoever she is, is on to them. Just before she turns around I see the shadow of a door open and close.

"Is it a mouse, or a mole?" She shines the flashlight around again, this time into corners and under tables before she locks in again on the monitor spewing out Leo's messages.

I don't miss this new hint: A mole is a spy. Lex and Kairos are about to get caught!

"Okay, game's up. Come out, before I call the police." She pauses, then says in a sly cat sort of voice, "Or a parent . . ."

With that, she unholsters her walkie-talkie and starts tuning in to another frequency.

"Go ahead." It's Dad.

"Possible security breach in your office, sir. Suspicious activity. You're getting security breach alerts. Before I call the police, I am wondering . . . could be a cyberattack. It's Firenze, sir. Over."

There's a hesitation in Dad's voice. "What's happening there? Over."

"It is my duty to report any potential breach. Protocol. You understand I am making this call preemptively since you are the lead investigator on OF—"

Dad cuts her off. "Yes, I understand. I will call you back on a secure line." The radio crackles off.

Next thing I see, Viola's talking on the phone in Dad's office—with the speaker on. What kind of security is that!

Dad's responding. "No, I am not aware of hackers, but I will check out the system again from this end."

"Thank you. You know," she says, "it is actually none of my business, sir, but you may be aware, Mr. Morton, every year after Take Your Child to Work Day, we get one or two of these smart-alecky kids who comes along and thinks—"

"I said I'd look into it, Viola," he interrupts, clearly angry now. "And as for smart alecks, my daughter could not possibly be involved. She has vanished into thin air, apparently something to do with a boy and a school project. And my wife is—"

"Oh, teenagers are the worst, Mr. Morton!" Viola suddenly comes alive at this. "Girl falls for a guy and it's all over! They're not coming home for dinner, not calling in that they're safe, and never where they're supposed to be! Or they're at some boy's house instead of their best friend's. I can tell you from firsthand experience!"

"Not sure this is helpful, Vi," I mutter.

"I should know," she continues. "I've done raised four of 'em on my own and—hold on—" She looks down at the monitor on Dad's desk. "Are you aware of any simulation programs that are supposed to be running overnight?"

"What's that? No, no simulations. *No one* is to touch any of the secure files on Operation Firenze. Let me check the remote network interface. Hold on, Viola . . ."

I can hear Dad's footsteps as he walks, then the sound of papers being shuffled around, presumably on his workbench. I try to picture the garage as I saw it in Dad's earlier conversation with Viola. What did I leave out of place that might make him suspicious? And wouldn't it maybe *actually be a good thing* if he figured out what I'd done?

I cross my fingers and shift my weight from one foot to the other, pondering the odds—figure it out, Jerry vs. don't figure it out, Jerry.

With his next utterance, I have my answer.

"The Operation Firenze manual—don't tell me, they've taken the—CHAAAARLEY! That girl is about to be grounded for life!"

And then in a calmer voice he says, "No, no need to call the police, Viola. I have a feeling it's no more mysterious than a science fair experiment run amok. My daughter will be answering to me on this one!"

That's when Viola completely changes her tune. "Then you do understand that I have to follow protocol, Mr. Morton. It's gotta be reported! I don't care if it's the good Lord himself! We have to answer to the FBI if any of this gets out."

Dad sounds stressed. "Um-hmm. Yes, I get it—protocol. Sure, you better believe that I'll be taking care of this report myself. No need to alert the FBI. Thanks, Viola."

The FBI?! Does that mean Dad could go to jail because of me?

Viola ends the call. "Humph. Thinking their kids are little angels. Untouchable. Well, I don't know that I trust Mr. Morton on this. I'm going to have to notify my supervisors, or there'll be hell to pay!"

I see her take one more exhaustive look around before leaving the premises, locking doors behind her.

At which point I see Kairos shaking a now-snoring Lex back to life.

"Whazzup? Hey, man! Don't rat me out. I didn't do anything. I'm—"

Kairos pulls Lexy up and starts dusting him off. "No need to worry, good signor. I am on your—team. I have seen your friends Carlotta and Billy. They will need your help!"

"Carlotta . . . you mean Charley? What are you talking about? Do you go to our school? What do you mean, you've seen Billy?"

"No time to explain. You must come with me before time runs out."

And before Lex can say "I'm already hip," Kairos reactivates the computer program that sent Billy on his journey until he and Lex both disappear into the vortex, and Bethy and I once again are subject to tornado-like winds.

"CHARLEY!" Lex calls. "You and your stupid disappearing *aaaact*. . . ." I hear him holler until I can hear him no more.

OMG. This is one science experiment run majorly amok. I'm in heaps of trouble in two time zones. My crime if I can't get out of here: witchcraft. And if I do: staying out past curfew, disappearing Billy and Lex, national security breach, and espionage.

Either option: a life sentence.

My life is so majorly out of control, things could hardly get worse.

Could they?

VIII.

DANGER! HUNGER!

"Where has Lexy gone?" Bethy asks, catching me by the shoulder.

I sigh. I am suddenly so-so-so tired. I wilt to the ground, even though I know we can't stop here. Not safe. And I know I should be worried about Billy and Lex too. Where they might have gone, or if they're even still alive. I take small comfort in knowing that Kairos seems to be the mastermind here. Or perhaps Leo's given him marching orders to set a plan in place—a plan hatched from the fertile imagination of the one and only Leonardo da Vinci. After all, Kairos has assured me he's just the apprentice.

Either way, I am left with the impression that Kairos knows what he's doing. Although, if he really understands how to manipulate space and time as easily as that, why wouldn't he have delivered me home by now?

I can't even think straight anymore. I haven't slept in half a millennium; no food of real sustenance has crossed my lips in at least as long. Mostly, I want to sleep.

"I dunno, Bethy," I say, letting out a yawn despite attempts to stifle it. "Do you think, maybe, there's somewhere we could grab a bite?"

Bethy gives me a determined look. "*Ah, si*," she says, with urgency quickening her voice. "We must get back to the *taverna*. Mamma will have made the food for tonight's banquet. Maybe there will be scraps left for us."

Even leftovers sound good. "*Si, si!* I could eat a horse!" I reply before realizing she might take that literally. "Not really. Kidding. No horses," I amend. "So, umm, how far is it to your place? I don't know that I can walk much farther."

"Not too far," she assures me, pulling me up by the hands. "*Viene,* Carlotta. By all means, we must get out of here before the world turns dark. The Carnival revelries will begin shortly—and soon the piazzas, *vie,* and back alleys will be flooded with masked revelers, fools, and thieves. It will no longer be safe for us to hide here."

Wrapped up in the drama at home, I'd barely noticed how fast night was descending. Even though we must be getting along into March, dark still comes pretty early—and here, dark is really dark.

Bethy's already walking, forcing me to hurry to catch up. After all, I don't even know my way by daylight, and in deepening twilight, everything's begun to look alike. For someone as directionally challenged as me, that's a serious disadvantage. I'd check to see if my phone can pick up even an echo of a GPS signal, but it's getting drained pretty quick. Now that night is nigh upon is, as the poets might say, there will be no way to harness the sun's power to recharge. That's gonna reduce my chances of listening in on the future.

Luckily, my tablet's still got quite a bit of juice, so once we get safely inside (and I use that term loosely) I'll be able to fire her up. I hope the livestream from home continues to deliver. Someday, when this is all history, I'll have to really figure out that whole mystery, but for the moment, I'm just grateful that it works.

Meanwhile, Bethy seems to be taking the long way home, what with all the twists and turns she's making. It's a wonder she doesn't lose me altogether as we dodge through crowds. I notice there are torchlights brightening the more populous streets, and people carrying lanterns in front of them. Compared to the neon-signed and headlight-washed fluorescence of streets back home, this world looks lit by fairy dust.

"Bethy, hold up!" I call out as I thread in and out of the crowd, narrowly missing setting my hair on fire by brushing too close to the torches. I'm running out of breath, and getting seriously delirious.

I'm thinking I oughta put up a warning sign by the time machine, in case anyone else decides to try this crazy adventure someday:

WARNING: TRAVEL OUT OF TIME MAY BE DANGEROUS.
PROCEED WITH CAUTION.
OR AT LEAST BRING FOOD.

I stop to catch my breath. Even when my body calls out for rest, my mind continues to tick away: *There are people here who want to hurt me. . . . Where's Leonardo, and is he helping with the Renaissance-engineering on the time machine? . . . FEED ME! . . . I want my mamma!*

It's hard to stay mindful and in the moment when you really are running from rattlesnakes.

Eyes on Bethy and keep moving. That's my new mantra.

But looking around, I've completely lost her. "Bethy? Elisabetta?"

"We will soon be home, Carlotta!" Bethy shouts from somewhere.

Home? Not likely. I squint through the dim twilight. A damp fog is closing in, but at least my immediate surroundings are beginning to look familiar. I can make out the clock tower above the Palazzo Vecchio. It's chiming the quarter hour. So I know it's fifteen minutes after something, but I'll have to wait a whole 'nother forty-five minutes to know the hour—unless they've somehow lit the clock face. Or the sands in the hourglass of my devices can also count up minutes and seconds.

I can barely make out the outline of the famous Duomo behind the palace—the dome of Florence's oldest standing cathedral—so if I am where I think I am, I know I'm not too far from other landmarks I've already stumbled on: the Pitti Palace, just over the Ponte Vecchio—the bridge over the Arno. It's where I had my first encounter with Bethy, the boys, and Wilbur, and it seems like an eon ago—which reminds me: Tonight, or five hundred years from tonight, *la mia mamma* is supposed to play there with the National Symphony. If she's not too sick. Wish I could text her—but even in the best of times, Mamma doesn't text. And this is definitely not the best of times.

I wish I knew what was going on with her! And to let her know I'm nearby, in spirit at least. I imagine I hear the strains of our musical composition, "Leo," that Mamma's rearranged for the orchestra. They're premiering it here in Firenze tonight. Or that future night. Ironic, isn't it?

The crowd is thinning in the Piazza della Signoria, if that's where I am. Families scurrying home for supper. I imagine they will all be sitting down to their pasta dinners. The Renaissance version of that, anyway. I can practically smell the oregano! I wish I were one of them!

"Elisabetta, *dove?*" I shout for her, fighting back tears when she doesn't respond. I'm done trying to keep up with the gazelle-like Bethy. In the semi-quiet of the evening, I sit down on one of the fountains, and to calm myself, I begin to hum a tune, Mamma's and mine.

"Hmmm, hmmm, da-da-da-dah; da-da-da-dah; hmm, hmm . . ."

Feeling better, I stop . . . but the music continues. I'm hearing snippets of instruments—like an orchestra tuning up.

Then, an anxious voice: "Call me back with good news, Jerry. It's gonna be alright. She's gotta be alright."

"Mamma!" I shout, despite myself, casting my eyes wildly around the piazza. "Mamma, it's me! Your Carlotta!"

If any of Lorenzo's people were to recognize me at this moment, I wouldn't even care.

My tablet—surely that's where the noise is coming from. What if they *could* hear me?! I start singing into the tablet again when, suddenly, I hear sirens in the background. They seem to be getting louder.

There, not here.

No sirens will blare out over this piazza for another 450 years!

I pull out my tablet, and I see her. Mamma! She's not at the Pitti Palace, where the orchestra must be tuning up, but in a clinic of some sort. She's dressed in her black skirt and white blouse, looking concert-ready, and sitting, alone, on a hospital bed. She's cradling her cell phone in between her open palms and talking into them, like a prayer.

"We would've heard something if—"

"I'm okay Mamma!" I yell into my tablet. There, Mamma's worried about me, and here I am worried about her, and I can't do a danged thing about it.

"If you're in Florence, I will find you if it's the last thing I do, Charley. I wish I'd given you a phone with international roaming."

Hah! International roaming. That's funny, I think grimly.

"Call me back, Jerry, dammit! Why does something like this have to happen when I'm a million miles from home? What have you gotten yourself into, *Carlotta!*"

At that moment, I see none other than her friend Giuliana waltz into the hospital room.

"Gwen, darling . . . are you okay? How would I have known of your illness? Luckily, my dear friend, your concertmaster, had the presence of mind to call me after you passed out. Have they figured out what's wrong?"

"Giuliana, there is absolutely nothing wrong with me that finding my lost daughter wouldn't fix! Jerry called and said—then there was a young stagehand who showed me video—and I passed out . . . and next thing I know, they are carting me away by ambulance to the hospital, where I am beamed with X-rays, assaulted by ultrasound, and subjected to all kinds of unnecessary medical tests."

I hear Giuliana tut-tutting.

"Jules, I assured them I was fine, but you know, an American musician on tour—they're taking no chances."

Yeah, tell me about it, I think, a little resentful. An American musician comes to Florence and gets the star treatment. Her unknown teen daughter, not so much. Still, I'm glad they're taking care of her. It does seem to me that Mamma's looking a little perkier.

Giuliana sits down on the bed next to her. "I was able to reach Jerry and let him know I'd check up on you. He seemed distracted, but, of course, I'd expect that under these circumstances. But I'm more concerned about you. Is it Carlotta that gave you such a shock, Gwen?"

"I'm fine, fine. But I'm telling you, Jules! Some stagehand came over to me at the Pitti while we were rehearsing. He claimed to know where she is—and to assure me she is fine. He gave me his phone and well—I saw her, Giuliana. *I saw Charley, in Florence, with my own eyes,* wearing some kind of, well, a Halloween costume is the only thing I can figure! Giuliana, I am sure she is here."

"But how—? Wouldn't Carlotta know to contact you if she were here?"

Before Giuliana has a chance to ask any more perfectly logical questions, a doctor walks into the room carrying her own tablet, no doubt to review Mamma's health records. Her English is heavily accented.

"Signora Morton, fortunate news! All goes well. We will be releasing you in time to get to the concert hall. The tests, they came back negative, and we've been able to speak with your doctors in the States. But given your condition, I'm not sure you should be taking on so much travel after this. Your doctors at home mentioned that, given your age, at some point they expect you will need to be put on bed rest."

"Her age? Bed rest?" Something is wrong, I knew it! I feel a knot growing in the pit of my stomach. "But I thought you said she was good to go!" I complain loudly to the unhearing doctor on the other side of my tablet.

It will do me no good to get upset here, under the circumstances. "*Calmo*, Charley," I tell myself. I shift forward on the edge of the fountain, feeling a little wobbly. Mamma needs me!

"Wait, Gwen. Is there something you're not telling me?" Apparently, Giuliana is thinking the same thing.

Mamma shoots the doctor a familiar "Don't say anything!" look, but apparently the *medico* is not on the same wavelength.

"Well, we do want to make sure these babies benefit from a healthy, full-term pregnancy, of course!"

Babies? What babies? Mamma's *pregnant*?! What way is this to break such monumental news to your one and only *baby*!

I jump to my feet with renewed urgency. Now would be a convenient time to make a temporal leap forward. If only I could click my heels and show up in my own backyard.

But I know firsthand that time travel is not so easy. I sit myself back down, a leg on each side of the fountain, with one foot barely dangling above the water line, trying to make sense of this situation. I vaguely wish I could take the boot off my gimpy foot and soak it in the fountain, but I have to be ready to run. I begin to rock back and forth, the tension propelling my perpetual motion.

But then, what unstoppable force should right this minute be flying headlong toward me, but Carolina.

"*Aiyee, Tcharr-li!* You must come with me, *Tcharr-li*, we have not a moment to lose. You must come!"

And at impact, this human mini-cannonball blasts us both off the stone wall and into the drink.

IX.
WORLDS COLLIDING

"Now you've done it, Carolina!" I shout. I pick my head up out of the fountain, only to see her flailing in the water, struggling to find her footing. When she begins choking and gasping for air, I realize she must have taken some water in the nose.

"Carolina!" I immediately reach for her. The water isn't deep, but I guess if you're not expecting it, even a deep bathtub could be a little scary. I grab her by the upper arms and, with an effort, manage to pull her up to standing.

"You okay, little one?" I ask. Lucky I took a lifesaving class and learned the Heimlich maneuver at our neighborhood pool last summer. I quickly haul myself back up to perch on the edge of the fountain, pulling her sodden body over my lap, and turn her head down to pound her on the back to clear all the water out of her lungs.

"Thank goodness. You're breathing again!"

She's soaked, shivering, and looking like a drowned rat, poor thing. I take my sleeve to help dry that little face. She starts barking like a seal, and I realize my wet sleeve can't dry anything and we laugh together. Even with the laugh, I can see she's in a bit of shock.

"C'mon, Carolina. You'll be okay," I assure her, although I feel far from certain of that myself.

'Cause when I stop to think about it, I've been through quite a shock myself in the past five hundred years and eighteen hours or thereabouts. My world's turned literally upside down.

Now, this new revelation that I'm soon gonna be a big sister! Wonder how many extra sibs that will be. The doctor said babies—*plural*. So, like, two . . . three . . . seven? I will soon be outnumbered!

I wonder how long it takes for PTSD symptoms to show up.

No, I have to keep my wits about me. Carolina's dragging, and I realize I've already begun thinking of *her* as a little sister.

"Let's get you home, little girlfriend," I say, pulling her to standing and helping both of us out of the water. "I've lost Elisabetta. Can you show me the way?"

But Carolina still has that glazed look in her eyes. That's when I notice that Translator's come off and is floating atop the water. On top of everything else, she can't understand me. I quick fish it out, praying that Kairos, or Leonardo, or whoever designed this advanced technology had the foresight to make it waterproof. Of course, the fake-fur covering is soaked. Water streams out of the earpieces: not a hopeful sign.

But most disconcerting of all—what if all my prophetic e-devices have suddenly become sunken treasures? I fish out my tablet; a quick peek indicates the battery is on life support—even the hourglass timepiece that's replaced the digital clock seems stuck at half full. My phone, luckily, is in the backpack that was at my feet before I was rocket-propelled underwater. Maybe there's still a chance!

"*Viene, bambina,*" I say in my most comforting voice.

"*Tcharr-li, andiamo!* We have no time to waste!" At that, the jumping bean takes off again.

"Wait, where are you going?" I ask, fitting the dripping Translator back around my ears. She turns briefly to wave me forward. I grab my backpack and make a beeline behind her.

"Slow down, Carolina! *Piano, grazie! Dove mi stai portando?*"

From the look of things, we are not going back to Signora Vincenzo's. In fact, it looks like we're on a road back out of town. What little torchlight is available is fading, and the jeweled and masked crowds that were gathering in the center of Firenze—ostensibly on their way to the Carnevale festivities—are thinning.

Carolina hastens ahead. It's all I can do to keep up, and keep from bumping into things as the mist lifts to unveil a glistening new moon.

"Wait, Carolina—aren't we going to find Bethy?"

"*Si, signorina,*" she replies solemnly, slowing down a little. At least I know we're back to speaking the same language!

"But this doesn't look like the way to Vincenzo's."

"We must stop along the way. For friends." There's a note of mischief in her voice.

"Friends! My only friends here are you and Bethy. And Leonardo, although I'm not sure I can call him a 'friend,' exactly. I mean, he's old!"

"*Tcharr-li,* you must understand. To you, we are all old!"

I reflect on this. "That's awfully smart of you, Carolina!"

She grins.

"Speaking of smart—how could Bethy have known to send you to find me?"

"There are no secrets in Firenze. Surely you have observed this, *Tcharr-li!*"

"You can say that again! I bet there are spies everywhere, shadowy people listening, hiding deep in doorways and back alleys to track our every move."

"Oh, you will not be discovered here. And Ser Leonardo, he always knows where to find you!" she replies.

Leonardo knows where to find me? And now, we're meeting friends . . . a group that apparently does not include Leonardo or Bethy.

What kind of wild goose chase is this?

Soon it becomes clear, even as the shadows lengthen around us, and the tall cypress trees take on the spooky appearance of dark, silent sentinels. She is leading me back to the field where I made my not-so-graceful entrance—was that just yesterday?

Instinctively, I stop and crouch low, protecting my head with my arms: a flashback to cannonballs flying. Maybe I'm already showing symptoms of trauma.

"We must not stop yet, *Tcharr-li*," she implores, prying my hands off my head and pulling me to my feet, which I promptly trip over. "There is nothing to fear—look!"

I cautiously open one eye, and see that just up the hill is a stone fence with the top of a stone cross poking above it.

"What the . . . ?"

"*Mwuh! Mwuh, mwuh mwuh! Mwuh mwuh mwuh?*"

I can't quite place the voice: water in my ears. I take off Translator, swallow hard, and poke a finger in each ear, hopping first on one foot, then the other, and shaking my head to clear the water out.

"*Carlotta! Carolina.* I have a message for you from da Vinci."

I spin on my heel. "Kairos!" I yell. "You are a sight for sore eyes!" I rush up to give my friend a squeeze.

"Carlotta, please do not squeeze—"

But he returns my hug awkwardly.

But then I remember. "Say, wasn't that you I just saw with *mia madre* in that other Florence?"

He dismisses my entreaty. "I know of no other Florence than this one," he avers, and then brandishes a page out of Leonardo's folio; I'd recognize Leo's handwriting anywhere. I decipher his mirror writing with difficulty:

"Our life is made out of the death of others."

"Again with the cryptic notes," I say with as much sarcasm as I can muster under the circumstances. "What's this supposed to mean anyway, Kairos?"

"Were I to interpret from the vantage point of the future," he explains laboriously, "I might suggest you look for the maestro . . . *there.*" He gestures toward the high stone wall up the hill.

How did Kairos get that from Leonardo's message? I wonder. But my questions will have to wait.

We begin walking, Carolina dragging up the rear. The mist deepens as night descends. I shiver as the last vestiges of a warm March day weaken with the sun's disappearance.

"Wait, what? How come I didn't see that before?" I ask. We have reached a small, run-down cemetery on the outskirts of Florence. It's like a potter's field, the place where poor people are buried.

"You are invited to a ceremonial grave digging, Carlotta. It is an honor. Ser Leonardo will be performing his surgery."

"Surgery!"

"*Chirurgia! Va bene. Andiamo, Tcharr-li!*" Carolina chimes in excitedly, pulling me by the arm. Like this is something she's been looking forward to her whole life.

"Ah, but no, Carolina," Kairos cautions her. "You did well, but you are not here to escort Carlotta to the graveyard. You must come with me—we are to fetch some friends." Kairos grins at Carolina, punching her playfully on the arm.

She giggles at her brother's praise.

"Besides, we must get you dry clothes so you don't fall ill in the night air. Here, bambina! Kairos will make sure you don't catch any night air fevers."

He takes off his cloak and wraps it around Carolina.

I want to explain that night air doesn't cause any fevers, germs from viruses do. And you can't get them from being out of doors. But surely Kairos knows this!

"Leonardo will be meeting you here anon," he says. *"Buona fortuna!"*

"Why will I be needing good luck?" I inquire, but before he can respond, there's a scuffle of footsteps beyond the graveyard gate.

"Ah, *buona sera!*" a familiar voice behind me greets us.

At this moment, a whistling Leonardo appears at the cemetery gate, gesturing. He is carrying a weirdly shaped wooden spade with a metal edge, undoubtedly something of his own design.

"Viene con me, Carlotta," he says. "I know you to be curious about life. I invite you also to observe, with me, the body without life."

"Uh, no thanks, Leo," I reply. "If you don't mind, I think I need to change my clothes, before I catch my death."

The irony is not lost on me that I've just told Kairos one can't get sick from cold. But cemeteries, and plague deaths, and viruses . . . that may be another story altogether.

"Our life is made out of the death of others," repeats the maestro/artist/scientist.

I'm not so sure of that anymore.

But Leonardo, never at a loss for words, is on a roll. "Every loss which we incur leaves behind it vexation in the memory, save the greatest loss of all, that is death, which annihilates the memory together with life."

That's when I start to shiver in full. I whisper, *"Andiamo, Carolina?"* hoping I can bring along an ally to keep me company. "Kairos, can she come?"

Carolina seems positively gleeful at the prospect. *"Si, Tcharr-li! A me!"*

"No!" Leo glares pointedly in her direction. "The grave will fall in upon him who digs it."

This makes me mad. "Just you wait a gosh darn minute, maestro. Who are you saying's going to fall into a grave?

"You cannot risk that, Carlotta," notes Kairos, "else your timeline would not show you alive in your own century. The time travel paradox, remember?"

This sounds like more of Kairos's mysterious mumbo jumbo. If I were thinking more clearly, I might be able to figure out how to put this into context, but my now illogical amygdala is suddenly running away with the idea of even more dangers we may be about to embark on.

As Carolina stomps her feet in protest, Kairos puts the final nail in that, ahem, coffin, as it were. "And paradox is also why Carolina may not come with you."

"Wait, where are you going?" I ask, as it appears Kairos is taking Carolina away.

"To change clothes, *Tcharr-li*," she says. "But do not fear. You are not alone!"

"But I'm soaked too!" I protest. "If you'll just be patient for a moment, Leonardo, I could change and come back—"

"Patience serves as a protection against wrongs as clothes do against cold," Leonardo says, as if that solves everything. We halt abruptly.

"Hah! I don't know if I can take any more shocks. . . ." I feel a panic attack coming on, but it seems the forces of history are working to test my steadfastness. "Well, if I must, I must. . . ." As Leonardo swings open the heavy gate, I put a hand on the wall to steady myself.

"Breathe, Charley. You know you can do this," I tell myself. "Nothing to be afraid of here."

As I'm mumbling this mantra, Kairos practically pushes me inside the gate. "It is getting late. And the maestro awaits."

X.
Ghosts and Goblins and Ghouls, Oh My!

Leonardo grabs my arm and pulls me hastily inside. There are holes dug for new burials, rough-hewn tombstones lying on their sides, cross-engraved slabs—and bodies—strewn about casually, as if some mass catastrophe has decimated the population with not enough stone carvers and gravediggers to take care of their dead.

All the most famous Medicis up to this time are buried elsewhere—it is before the crypt in Lorenzo de' Medici's own chapel, after all, is constructed. I refrain from mentioning this to Leonardo, remembering that his chapel was constructed by none other than his archrival, Michelangelo. Under the circumstances, I don't want to upset the maestro.

"So, what are we doing here?" I ask, hoping to appear smart and businesslike, even if I'm not feeling it. I've often visited the cemetery at home where my grandfather is buried, but this place, with its ancient bones, is way freakier.

"Bright girl that you are," begins Leo, "I thought this place might interest you. From a medical point of view," he adds.

"Umm?" I look around furtively.

Leonardo stoops down beside one freshly dug grave, picking up smooth, rounded stones from the earth alongside the grave, placing one on top of the crude headstone. He looks reverently upon it and gestures.

I stoop on the other side and read: Piero, 1387–1425; Caterina, 1410–1438. They died young. My heart catches when I read Bambina, 1490–1492. This baby must have just died. I let my finger trace the names and dates carved into the stone.

There's a sliver of a moon above the horizon now, and a cool breeze sends prickles down my arms.

Or could it be the chilling breath of ghouls and ghosts?

I get the feeling that there are definitely spirits here, beyond me and Leonardo. But to admit that would not be fitting for a scientist such as myself. Or Leonardo (though he might not understand "science" as we do, meaning a system for understanding the physical world). But, surely, "scientist" is what he is.

Leonardo pulls out a wooden box that looks pretty beat up. It is closed with a simple metal hasp and two locks, one with a combination and one with a key.

I freeze, not knowing what to expect, though I'm itching to get my fingers on that lock—we learned to pick them in a hack-a-thon with Girls in Technology, an afterschool club I belong to.

"Ecco," he says. "Here it is." As if that explains everything.

Leo then produces a candle inserted into a holder and gives it to me to hold while he lights it. Amid the flame flickers, I note numbers carved into the wood. Leo tells me it's his nightlight—as the candle burns down, it marks the hours until dawn.

Leonardo pulls a chain off from around his neck—it holds the key. He unlocks the lock and dials the combination. Slowly, he raises the lid and motions me over to spy a canvas cloth wrapped around a ball-shaped object. I strain closer as he peels back the canvas to get a look at whatever treasure it might contain.

"Holy Moses!" I gasp. Inside is a human head. Not just the bleached bones of a skull; it looks like whoever the actual person was is still there, with skin, brown, withered and dry, like leather. Embalmed. Open eyeballs are staring at me.

"Not Moses, I'm afraid. Some poor wretch who's died of a pox, no doubt."

Leonardo reaches in to lift the head aloft in his left hand, peering closely into its eyes.

I begin to laugh uncontrollably, a break from the anxiety of this moment, this evening, this day out of time. Leo shushes me loudly, afraid, perhaps, that I will wake the dead. Which cracks me up even more.

Gasping for air, I go for the dramatic. "Alas, poor Yorick, I knew him well!" I declaim, hand over my heart and putting on my best British accent.

"*Yorrrrick?*" asks Leonardo, rolling the "r" in that way of his.

"Why, yes, it's a line from Shakespeare, a play called *Hamlet.*"

Leonardo lifts an eyebrow. "A play. This is perchance a pageant of some sort? And this . . . Shake-*spearrra?* He is a friend of yours?"

I laugh, despite myself. "No. He's from England." We wouldn't read *Hamlet* until ninth grade, but I had seen it on stage at the Shakespeare Theatre Company in Washington last spring (or *will* see in about five hundred years, if I manage to hack the second leg of this journey!).

But the maestro has moved on to other, more present, concerns. Engrossed in his prized bones, Leonardo caresses the skull like a mother might stroke the head of a baby.

"You see, Carlotta, this is how we learn the art of anatomy. Very useful to an artist—or a healer. To see nature as it is, the eye must connect to the brain. I have dissected both, in order to draw these connections. I followed the entire path of vision through the pupil and the lens to the optic nerve—and from there into a special cavity in the brain. The eye

makes an upside-down impression of what it sees, which is reversed in the brain."

He points to my eyes, which I, of course, cannot see. "Here forms, here colors, here the character of every part of the universe are concentrated to a point; and that point is so marvelous a thing!"

It sounds poetic, in an old Florentine sort of way. I'd almost say that Leonardo has some of the Bard in him. Or, if you believe that time flows in only one direction, then Shakespeare was channeling da Vinci.

"Now," he exclaims breathlessly, "can you not see that the eye embraces the beauty of the whole world?"

"Umm . . . er . . . well . . ." I'm thinking of Leo's future painting, *Mona Lisa*. As I recall, the maestro won't begin to paint the portrait of this woman with the mysterious smile, and the eyes that seem to follow you as you stare, for another ten years or so. His pioneering techniques in painting her come from a scientist's understanding of vision, anatomy, chemistry, and color to create a virtual reality. Those eyes that the whole world will embrace as beauty were created by a genius who saw the whole as greater than its parts.

He offers me the shrunken head. "Would you care to examine it?"

I have a special fascination with brains, and I'm wondering if Signor Mummy, or whoever Leonardo's holding, still has one. I've only seen an actual human brain once before—the mother of one of the kids in my class, a neurosurgeon, brought an actual brain to school one day. I remember touching it (I have to touch everything! I can't help it; touching is part of how I understand the physical world) and thinking it felt like Jello, a little squishy and shivery.

But this one is different: a dead person looking up at me as if he's still alive. I wonder what killed him. "Is his brain still intact, do you think?" I ask.

Leo produces a sharp carving knife. "Let us see. Carlotta, would you do the honors?" he asks, holding the carved hilt of the knife in my direction. I can just barely see the glint of the silver blade in the candlelight.

"Oh, no!" I shriek, stepping back. "I'm really bad with knives!" As should be well understood by now, I am something of a klutz.

"How will you become an *artista*, Carlotta, if you do not learn to handle the tools?"

I hadn't actually been thinking of becoming an artist, given that my talents lie elsewhere than with the brush—or the knife. But as I gently take Leonardo's knife in hand, I recognize that learning the tools of any trade is important. And if this superstitious world for any reason becomes my permanent place of residency (please, please, please help

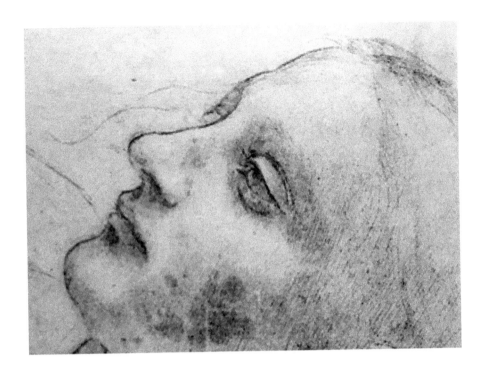

me figure out how to activate the time machine from this primitive past) . . .

"Ooph!" My hand is shaking so hard I lose my grip. I watch, as in seeming slow motion, the knife hilt drops out of my hand and the blade stakes itself into the ground, barely missing my big toe in the process. I start to freak out.

"*Attenzione, cara ragazza!*" Patiently, Leonardo picks the knife up again and hands it back, this time, careful to hold his hand over both of mine until I have a firm grip.

I look up quizzically. "Are you expecting me to, like, open up this dude's head?"

"How else to see if a brain remains inside his skull, Carlotta?" He spreads out his cloak over a flat stone slab that must cover some poor dead soul, and sets the skull lovingly down.

I look around nervously; no one is here but me and Leonardo. And the dead.

"Breathe, Charley!" I command myself silently as Leo again tightens his hands around mine and the blade handle and raises it to leverage a sharp stab into the skull. "Don't forget to breathe."

Curiosity overcomes my fear. I shrug Elisabetta's cloak back to free my arms. I take one more deep breath.

"Carlotta!" shouts a familiar voice.

I drop the knife again with a start. It clangs against the stone. My heart's hammering in my ears.

"Who's there?! Kairos, is that . . . ?"

"Art is never finished, only abandoned," Leonardo ruefully observes. "Time is long enough for those who use it. Carlotta, I can see the time is not yet for you to learn the art of dissection." He carefully picks up the knife again and, this time, sheathes it.

I can't even hear him. "What kept you so long?" I blurt out at Kairos. "No, wait, don't tell me. I already know. You've been taking Carolina to get changed!"

Carolina, newly dressed in some courtly costume, pops out from behind Kairos, as if she has been waiting to make a grand entrance. "Ta-da! Ready for *Magnifico*'s masquerade ball."

Kairos grins. "That is partly so, you see. But perhaps you do not know everything, madonna!"

And what happens then, *cara amici*, is nothing short of unreal. Kairos magically produces an antique (this being a relative term, of course) cell phone from his pouch.

And with that bit of presto chango, in from behind the graveyard gate saunters . . . Billy?!

"Billy?" I shout. "What—? How—? OMIGOD, Billy, is it really you?!" It feels so good to say his name.

"Hey, Charley," he says in all his geeky normalcy, standing there in his baggy, too-short sweatpants, white socks, sneakers, and a Washington Nationals cap under his hoodie.

"Billy, Billy, Billy. I have never been so happy to see anyone in my life!" I run up to give him a hug. And as I drape my sopping, frumpy frock–adorned arms around him, I get a funny feeling in the pit of my stomach . . . and this time I don't think it's from being hungry.

"Yuck. You're all wet!" he says, as he peels me away gruffly.

Billy seems shaken up, of course. And laden down with a lumpy army-green duffel bag.

"Yeah, well. It's an unbelievably long story, Billy!"

XI.
WE ARE NOT IN OZ

Billy takes off his glasses. His eyes, aglow with starlight, are beautiful.

"So, you wanna fill me in on some of the details here, Charley? You have no idea how many people back home are worried about you!"

"You came. For me!" I exclaim.

"Yeah, for you. It wasn't for your Savonarola, that's for sure!"

"Wow." I feel my face flush. Why should I suddenly feel flustered—it's just Billy! I hastily file away the confusion; this is no time for sentimentality.

"But how—?"

"I copied that formula, Charley—the one you used to activate the time machine in your Dad's workshop! The Qualia Rosetta? Sheer genius!"

"I swear, it wasn't me. It appeared out of thin air! Or—" It's then I notice Kairos's eyes twinkling. "Or was that the work of Signor Just-in-Time, here?"

"*Al suo servizio, Signor Vincenzo!*" Kairos does the courtier's bow. "And this is my little sister, Carolina," he says, graciously introducing her. Carolina gives Billy a high five.

"I taught her that!" I point out with pride.

"But as for the formula, I assure you, I am but Leonardo's humble messenger. I merely carry forward the formulations made by the maestro."

My feeling of frustration is growing. Nothing here is as it seems, and I feel like I want to scream! Instead, I reach up and knock Kairos upside the head. "So you mean Leonardo could have sent me back before now?"

"Not likely, signorina. He did not have the key without the knowledge you and Billy are able to impart! The folio Billy carries with him in his sack. *Operazione Firenze.*"

Like magic, Billy flips through a booklet rendered in mirror writing as Kairos continues.

"And your tablet and battery to harness the energy of the sun!"

Leonardo, having laid Yorick on a nearby gravestone, walks over and is now scrutinizing Billy's getup. "Another refugee from your century, I take it, Carlotta?"

"Billy, I present you Leonardo da Vinci," I pronounce proudly.

Billy is momentarily speechless. "So it's true! You're the great Leonardo. . . ."

"Of course. And I am guessing you have my formula and the key in your possession, Ser Vincenzo?

Billy looks puzzled. Of course . . . he has no idea what Leo is saying! Even though he took intro Italian last term, and even though he's off-the-charts genius in math and engineering, he's really not so hot with languages.

But then Kairos steps over and hands something to Billy. "Signor, a gift. These will help you communicate in any language across time."

"Dude, you're an inventor too!" Billy exclaims, fist bumping Kairos, before sticking what look like earbuds in his ears. Seems Kairos has modernized Translator since we first met. Those are way cooler than my purple fur-covered headphones.

"He's asking you about the formula, and the extra key, Vincenzo," I remind Billy once he's tuned in.

"How do you . . . I mean, what do you know about . . . ?" he asks Leo.

"Simple observation, my boy," says Leonardo. "You come from a distant time carrying a large sack with what Carlotta tells me is a zipper. Ingenious trick, by the way. Would that I had the tools . . ."

"But the formula?"

"How would you have cracked the code without it?!" Leonardo points out reasonably enough. "So, have you worked out how to reverse it? I gather Carlotta needs to return to your time period, pronto."

"Yeah, pronto," I echo.

"*Si*, well, I might have it. . . ." Billy pauses just long enough to tell me that's not the whole story.

Leonardo strokes his beard, as if assessing the situation. "Perhaps I can help find a solution. Must go back to my drawing board."

Yorick now forgotten, the great da Vinci takes off under the gleam of a million stars.

"Do not forget, Ser Leonardo," Kairos calls out after him, "that tonight is the Carnival Ball. *Magnifico* will be expecting you to sing and play for his guests."

"Of course," comes back the fading voice of the master of everything. "The evening should be most entertaining. And I hope Carlotta will join me."

As Leonardo walks away, I take a moment to regain my footing, because overload does not begin to describe my mental state. My mom being pregnant is such new news that I'm not even sure how I feel about it. Except that it's weird for a teenager and only child, whose parents are

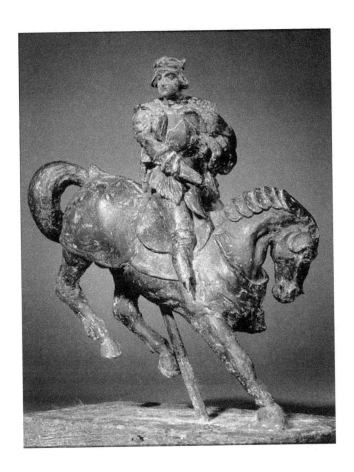

in their mid-forties, to suddenly be expecting to be a big sister.

"Billy, not that you aren't a sight for sore eyes, but—but—" I find myself stammering. "But I was hoping, maybe, well . . . I'm worried about, you know, stuff at home, and, um . . ."

Billy looks a little dejected. "We're gonna get home, Charley. I'm here to get you home!"

"If it were only that easy," I say.

Kairos smiles as he reaches into Billy's backpack and pulls out the Horse and Rider maquette. "Eureka!"

"Oh, thank God, the statue didn't break! I knew it had to somehow be 'mission critical.' But where's the matching key, dude?" Billy asks, as he reverently takes the Horse and Rider sculpture away from Kairos, who starts digging back in his pouch. "You know, Charley, the golden compass." Billy elaborates. "This one seems to lock snugly inside a slot on the Horse and Rider maquette. Perhaps it contains some code that can only be unlocked when the time is right? Anyway, I deduced that you need the pair to reverse the arrow of time—or, that is, to shoot it forward again."

I nod, trying to think this through carefully, but my head aches. "How . . . you know, I read your comment on my blog. I could see lots of things going on at home while—well, that is, before my tablet got waterlogged." I lift my cloak to check the tablet again. Still dead. "Dad's gonna be spittin' mad!" I say unhappily.

All this time, Carolina has been prancing between us, happy to have us all in one place. "I told you, you must come, *Tcharr-li*, to meet your friends!" she sings.

"Hey, little one," I say, remembering suddenly. "We've got Billy, but where's Bethy?"

"Elisabetta?" Kairos questions, on guard. "*Dove* Elisabetta, Carolina?"

Carolina peers into the darkness, as if Bethy must be hiding there. "'Betta!" she calls out. "Perhaps she is waiting for us to find her?"

"Bethy's here?" This from Billy. "What the—"

"No, not our Bethy," I start. "Remember, Carolina, she is preparing for tonight's Mardi Gras banquet, at the Palazzo Medici. Where we now know Leonardo will also be in attendance. A command performance for Lorenzo de' Medici himself!"

"Aha, so he said. But didn't he also invite you to join in the music-making, Charley?" Billy asks, suddenly showing a mischievous grin. "Then you might be needing this!"

He slowly reaches into his duffel bag, as if to taunt me with anticipation. I step in closer to sneak a peek; he turns and backs away so I can't see what it is.

Carolina is dancing a jig around Billy, trying to see what he's hiding. "*Fantastico!*"

"Ta-da!" Billy turns around, and there in his hands, he holds my precious violin and bow!

"My God, Billy!" I take my instrument reverently from his hands. "How could you ever—how did you know to bring my violin?"

Billy has a huge grin on his face.

I inspect carefully—strings, wood, neck, frets; it's completely intact. Probably could use tuning. I should check the tone, I think. But here and now, instead, on impulse, I plant a big fat kiss on Billy's cheek.

Billy's face goes red. "Aww, man. Germs, Charley!" But he doesn't wipe off my kiss. "And you're still soaking. Here, take my fleece. Maybe it will help."

He starts to pull his big sweatshirt over my shoulders, and I can't help but hug him. For just an instant, I melt into the warmth of his body, but I don't dare to look at him.

"*Grazie, mio ragazzo,*" I say shyly, accidentally using an Italian word for boyfriend.

Which wakes me up. "Hey, wait! Kairos, do you know what's happened to Lex?"

Billy looks puzzled. "I left him at your dad's, er, office. Did something happen to him?"

But before Kairos can clue us in, Carolina's pulling me by the hand and prancing off. Her teeth are chattering, whether with excitement or cold, it's impossible to know.

"At *Magnifico*'s palazzo you can put on suitable costumes, *Tcharr-li.*

Tua e Bee-ly e Kairos. Like me. Elisabetta will know to meet us there."

"*Si.* We must hurry," Kairos chimes in. "Maestro Leonardo is expecting us!"

"*Eh, bene*, no matter. We're off to see the Wizard!'" I sing brightly. Buoyed by hope, I hold Carolina's hand in my left, and take Billy's in my right, and skip off merrily in the direction Kairos is leading us.

But this is not Oz.

XII.
ANOTHER COUNTY HEARD FROM

We pause for breath on a hilltop with a view of Florence below. It looks like Lorenzo's guards have lit lanterns on poles around several of the central piazzas. The city seems so small from here!

We can hear Mardi Gras revelers hollering and howling—celebrating early, no doubt. The Arno glints steely under the moon, stars, and torches along its banks.

On what I'm guessing is the Piazza della Signoria, there are gigantic fires blazing—so dangerous if they're uncontained, I think, and without a fire engine or hose in the town—until I realize we might actually be witnessing a verifiable bonfire of the vanities. These blazes sending up smoke from the burning of paintings, furs, books, and other earthly treasures are meant to terrify the populace—and us—into submission.

"So this is Florence at night!" Billy takes in the scenic overlook, eyes glowing softly. Then he looks at me. "And to get to see it here with you—this is way cool, Charley." He squeezes my hand and, shyly, I squeeze back.

Kairos knocks the Nationals hat off of Billy's head to place it on his own. "Hush, lovebirds! We do not have time for spectator sports here. We must make haste to my master's studio if we are to keep you out of danger."

Before I can protest that we are definitely not lovebirds, I hear a loud thud nearby, then a man's voice, groaning. Is Leonardo back out testing weapons tonight?

Billy tenses, hyper-alert at every strange sound. And trust me, tonight, they are all strange. He drops my hand and spins around, whispering, "What in the world was that?"

"Banditos, no doubt!" Kairos replies, and I nod, remembering my own not-so-grand entrance, with bandits and gypsies on my heels in hot pursuit.

"They are known to prey on strangers. Wait here. And no matter what you hear, just wait for my signal that it is safe." Kairos points to a thicket at the woods' edge. "Carolina, keep still. And stay close to Carlotta."

Kairos begins walking toward the unidentified sound while Billy and I pull Carolina behind the bushes. Burrs and thorns are our armor. I can see how Billy's trembling. We listen in silence until Kairos's footsteps disappear down the hill. A cat dashes between us, and Billy jumps again.

"*Shh*," I urge, pulling him back from the clearing. The wait seems interminable, until we hear footsteps again, and what sounds like two voices, climbing back up the hill. Billy peeks out cautiously while I pin Carolina against me for safety.

"E man . . . you appear, *come si dice*? Lost." Kairos's voice—but has he found friend or foe?

"No kidding. That was some ride, man!"

"Billy, do you hear what I hear?" I whisper. I peep around the bushes cautiously.

"Lex!" we say in one voice. I slap Billy a high five. Of course, this being Carolina's new favorite game, she waves her palms in the air for a slap from each of us.

I start to jump out, but Billy holds me back. He whispers, "Remember Kairos's warning. . . . This may be some kind of trap."

"Yes, we have seen many strange apparitions today." Kairos is all *calmo*, like this kind of thing happens here all the time. "You are the third."

That would be us: three ghosts of Mardi Gras future. Quieter now, I watch the two shadows nearing, and there's no doubt about it—Lex has made the leap.

Carolina has kept still all this time. I'm proud of her. But hearing her brother and a new stranger—it's all she can do not to pop up and greet them. I put a finger to my lips and squeeze her shoulder. For my part, Lex represents some uncomfortable unfinished business. I don't want to give us away by talking aloud right now.

"Where the hell is this, anyway?" Lex demands.

"No, not hell at all: *Firenze, in Italia*. You see?"

"Whoa. Are those working cannons?" Lex asks.

"The real deal," Kairos replies.

"It's like being in the Matrix or something."

At this point, Billy pokes me excitedly: "You know, Charley, this is the virtual reality game I've gotta get back home to design," he whispers.

And I'm thinking, yeah, fun to play; just not the life I signed up for.

"Italy? But why the weird costume?" Lex asks, giving Kairos the once-over.

"Really, you are in *Firenze*, man. And tonight is the Mardi Gras ball."

Billy's so fidgety now, he jumps out from the bushes, screaming like a banshee, despite Kairos not having given us the all clear. "Lex! Welcome to history!" he shouts, fist bumping a stunned Lex.

"Webhead?! What are you doing—what are we—you know, I was kinda mad when you disappeared, after that whole mix-up with Charley, and—" He stops. "Wait a minute. This whole thing is some big hoax, right? Like a mad trick or treat!"

"No trick, Lex. I swear! It's what I told you, the time machine—Charley found her Leonardo. And we've gone back with her. You know, the girl really is some kind of genius!"

I want to maximize the surprise, so I stay back, but from my hiding spot I can't help but beam. I mean this is Billy, teen braniac of all times, and he thinks *I'm* the genius. I hug Carolina with joy.

"Whattaya mean, gone back? Bad enough you tricked me into sneaking into Mr. Morton's office. And then, after you disappeared, that sausage of a security guard almost found me. . . ." He's silent again, as if taking it all in. "Although . . . come to think of it, this is way cooler than hiding in some creepy, suffocating office."

"Eh, bene, ragazzi," Kairos interjects. "*Cosa state aspettendo?*"

"Huh?" With Kairos switching to Italian, Lex is clearly confused.

"Lex, meet Kairos," Billy says by way of introductions. "Kairos is quite the man-about-time."

From my hiding spot, I can see Kairos doff his new Nats cap and draw a wide circle with his arm, ending with the cap against his heart in a deep bow. Confused, Lex reaches his hand out to bump fists and, mistaking the signal, Kairos hands Lex his earbuds.

"That's where I know you: You're that dude from the office!" Lex lets out an *I just got this* kind of whoop. "So, Billy-boy, while you were busy trying to find out how Charley managed to set the GPS and all that jazz, I'm back in the recording studio hearing this voice talking all Greek or something, with some kinda weapons-engineering design. And I'm watching that sausage guard-lady in Charley's dad's office, and you were, like, *POOF!*

"So, who are you, really, dude?"

"I have an *intern-ship* with Leonardo da Vinci!" Kairos says, glomming on to my original interpretation of his day job as Leo's apprentice.

"Yeah, right." Lex apparently has to stop and think about that a second.

"So, then, Kairos, old pal, old buddy," he continues. "For sure, we are here to liberate Charley, right? But, for the sake of, you know, knowing . . . can you just send me and Billy back the same way? You know, round-trip the GPS, and voila! 'Cause I really gotta get home or the parents are gonna slay me. And my bike's not even locked up!"

"I wish it were as easy as you say, *miei amici*. Ser Leonardo is the mastermind here. And it is his mind that is at work on the problem of your return. Unraveling such a complicated puzzle . . . Carlotta has been most enlightening on the mechanics."

I can see Carolina start to open her mouth, wanting to interject on my behalf. I clap my right hand over her mouth, with my left on her shoulder to remind her to keep still.

"Does Leo need our help?" Billy interrupts, cutting him short. Kairos can go on and on.

"*Si*. Assistance from you whiz goats," Kairos says, obviously meaning *whiz kids*.

Lex harrumphs. "Well, you, Webhead, I can understand. And if old Leo wants some pointers on playing outfielder, then I'm his man. But as for the science and tech stuff—that's outta my league."

Kairos keeps sending questioning glances back at me and Carolina, still squirreled away.

Obviously nervous, Lex keeps talking. "I mean, it's a visit *to the future* I've been aiming for—my future in the twenty-first century. Not some lame-o ancient history no one cares about."

True confessions! I hang back to listen in, seeing as how Lex is not so hung up on me after all—I mean, Lex deserves to suffer a little.

"*Eh, bene . . . solo uno problema . . .* Carlotta is under suspicion for witchcraft!" Kairos elaborates.

I can't hold my tongue any longer. Jumping out of my hiding place with Carolina in front of me, I charge, "Witchcraft my foot! Whatever happened to innocent until proven guilty!"

"Charley!" Lex looks stunned. I chuckle; I never thought I'd see Mr. Too Hot to Handle let down the attitude.

Billy chimes in to defend me. "Charley was worried to let you see her—'cause of that whole stupid 'kiss' thing."

"Yeah. Well. That," I choke out, feeling my face burning at the memory. "It's so not . . . whatever. But Kairos—answer me this: What evidence would they have against me that I couldn't disprove using reason in a court of law?"

Billy again: "Wait, do they even have civil courts in, what year are we here . . . 1492 Florence? We're talking the Inquisition! And Charley, news flash: your Savonarola . . ."

Savonarola. How could I forget. I look across the panorama of Florence again. The revelers are out in full force now. The flames in the middle of the Piazza della Signoria have dwindled into gray clouds of smoke. Which may soon be my fate as well.

"I'm afraid Billy has reason, Carlotta." Kairos shakes his head. "Reason will not triumph here. And the evidence? Look no further than your *tavoletta*. That alone is enough for the Inquisitors to find you guilty of witchcraft!"

"Tablet? You mean they think her tablet . . . ? Well, there's no time to waste, is there!" Billy declares. "We need the brain of all brains in on this. Kairos, can you take us to da Vinci?"

Carolina is getting agitated. "But we are late already. He will already be *al palazzo*. Elisabetta must there too. *Il Magnifico* does not like to be kept waiting!"

Kairos nods. "But to fool Lorenzo de' Medici and his guests, we must act the fools! A masked costume. As it happens, *fortuna* smiles upon you; such costumes will be yours for the choosing at the Mardi Gras ball."

Billy winks at me. "Dude, we can totally do this!"

Lex mutters unhappily. "Really. Could this day get any crazier?"

Billy ignores him. "Kairos, I will need Leonardo's help. And I may need to get a message back, er, forward to Bethy somehow—*our* Bethy, that is—before this night is through."

"Sending messages ahead? Fear not, young master. That is my specialty. I am Kairos, at your service."

"And you aren't the only one, Kairos," I remind them, punching Kairos on the shoulder. "My blogs . . ."

Kairos bows in my direction. "*Sì*, to your success, madonna!"

"Charley, how did you see what was going on with us at home?"

"The tablet. Some weird app. I thought you maybe rigged it, no? But it's too late. My tablet got drenched. My phone's alive, but it's running down its battery PDQ."

At the mention of the tablet, finally Lex seems to come alive. "You need a working tablet? Then maybe I am your man!" He pulls something out of his backpack. "I grabbed this at your dad's office from that crazy control room. Thought I'd use it to check on my fantasy team— and you can hardly get more fantastic than this league of weirdos."

"OMG, Lex. You're a genius!" Out of the corner of my eye I catch Billy shooting me a dirty look. "I mean, not actually a *genius*, but, a lifesaver, all the same. . . ."

Lex isn't listening to me, though, as he opens what must be the most super-duper, ultra-secure tablet the universe has ever known. I see it's got a U.S. government ID number and the code OF20201492 scratched into it, and in the back of my head, I have the sneaking suspicion that this could be considered a Snowden-level offense—he had to go into exile after stealing top secret info from the National Security Agency.

And even with my friends now on the scene, being in exile is what it feels like here, at the moment. But when you're faced with being burned at the stake and missing the birth of your newly expected soon-to-be siblings, somehow, exile in a Moscow airport with amenities like indoor plumbing and a food court, even if it only serves blini and borscht, sounds like the stronger option.

XIII.

TAKE HEART

"Let me see that!" Billy grabs the tablet and powers it on. A warning screen pops up about property for government use only and all that blah-blah-blah about no stealing. On this one, too, the clock digits morph into an hourglass. But the sands of time are running out.

Billy starts checking apps, with Kairos pointing out certain programs that could be helpful. And that's when I remember—Kairos is the original IT guy! Or is it Leonardo, as Kairos insists? I just don't have enough of a sense of the pecking order.

"Okay, I've got this!" I declare finally.

"Then I will leave it to you, madonna." Kairos once again takes that deep bow. "I must go assist Maestro Leonardo and see to your disguises. Carolina, please guide them to the Palazzo Medici once they have located the necessary information! I have the feeling Carlotta could lose herself even in the bright light of day, much less the chaos of this festival night."

And, like lightning, he is gone.

Lex still seems dazed. "What's with all the bowing and scraping? That Kairos is one weird dude."

Billy jumps in. "Let's keep our eyes on the goal. Hopefully, Leonardo's been configuring the mechanism to rejigger the original formula to shoot the arrow of time forward and figure out the fractals involved in mapping out space-time energy currents."

It's reassuring to hear him confirm what I've been thinking. "Then, with the web interface, we'll need to input GPS coordinates for Takoma Park, Maryland, and the year, adjusting for Earth shift, leap years, and any natural disasters in intervening years that may have shifted the gravitational field. And ta-da! We head for home."

"Roger that," Billy confirms, as I refresh the page. The video chat screen opens.

"Yeah, Roger that, whatever he just said. But first, anyone got some chow?" Lex asks, tapping his gut. "A burger would be nice, or even a few energy bars? Not sure I can withstand that G-force again without putting some protein in here."

Food! That's a sore subject with me. My empty stomach rumbles at the mention. "Not here. Maybe at the masquerade, Lex," I say hopefully. "Just, please, stay away from any stuffed pigs."

"Even, like, a ham sandwich?" he asks. "I'm thinkin' a little prosciutto and mozzarella on ciabatta bread—we are in, Italy, right? Can we order out, maybe?"

"When pigs fly," I say.

Billy snorts. "I'm with Lex. Just hold the mayo."

"Mayo!" I laugh. "Cute, Billy, but probs not so much."

Despite his own Italian ancestry, Billy Vincenzo is not much of a foodie.

"Whatever," he retorts. "But first, let's see if we can't phone home. . . ."

As we watch on the official government tablet, the scene that shows up doesn't look all that much like home. It's the inside of the Palazzo Pitti, where I saw Mamma earlier at rehearsal. The crowd filling the hall shows elegant-looking people dressed in regal costume, wearing Mardi Gras masks. They could be guests of the de' Medici family, except for the few bejeweled young women in jeggings and modern-day chopines. What my mom would call—in that mortifyingly old-school way of hers—clodhoppers.

Bethy the First, fashionista and YouTuber fashion-designer wannabe, would feel right at home in such a crowd.

I see the chairs and instruments arrayed on stage. I gasp. There's Mamma. She is wearing her own costume—the orchestra's traditional uniform: white blouse and a long black skirt. She's tied on a purple bandana with slits for eyes, Zorro-like. She does seem pale, sitting quietly on a folding chair, her violin on the chair next to her. And serene, somehow. An island of calm amid the hubbub of jittery, tuning musicians and frantic stagehands. I detect what might be evidence of a baby bump, but it could just be the drape of her skirt.

Looks like she's scanning missed calls, because she punches one.

At that moment, her friend Giuliana walks up next to the music stand, holding out a bottle of water. "Gwen, you must put this all out of your mind if you insist on playing the concert tonight!"

"I know, Jules. And I know it's no good worrying. But you're a mom. You know what it's like!" She puts up her hand as the phone presumably rings through. "Jerry?" Mamma begins hopefully. "Any news?" That's when I see her mouth quivering.

Giuliana puts an arm around Mamma's shoulders, but she shrugs it off and turns away. "She'll show up, Gwen. With a brain like that—Charley's always been a most resourceful child!"

"*Mio cuore!*" At which, my mom is starting to cry, mask and all.

Her heart! This tears mine apart. I bury my head in my arms. I haven't even been gone a millisecond in the scheme of human existence, and I'm already being displaced as the center of my parents' universe. And I'm not even talking about the time-space thing. My mom is having a baby! And what with that whole mommy-baby bonding thing, from oxytocin and other hormones that ensure parents think their babies are the most adorable things on Earth. I'm about to come in a distant third in her line of affection, losing to some burpy, drooly, poopy mini-aliens with giant heads and big eyes whose main redeeming value is in their billion-florin smiles.

"And when were you planning on breaking that news to me, Gwendolyn Morton!" I hiss.

"Hey, Charley!" Billy interrupts my new jealous obsession, tapping the screen of the tablet. "Isn't that, um, Kairos? And wasn't he here just a second ago? How the heck does he do that!"

I look, and there, indeed, is the "just-in-time" Kairos. He's resumed his stagehand role but now stands lurking in the background. He looks over uncertainly at my mom and her friend, as if wondering about interrupting their intimate tête-à-tête.

Finally, he walks over and picks up Mamma's violin and begins plucking a few rudimentary notes that sound suspiciously like the intro to "Leo," our original composition.

Mom jumps up, clearly ready to throttle him. No one messes with Gwen's priceless Amati!

"Young man, I don't know who you are or what you think you're doing, but this is the second time today—"

"Eh, signora! Prego . . . I am trying to explain—"

Giuliana jumps in between Gwen and Kairos before Mamma can hurt him. "Signor, prego! La donna is upset. Her health is fragile. You can surely appreciate that this is an extremely rare, vintage seventeenth-century instrument. The insurance alone—"

Not impressed with an instrument that will not be invented for, like, another half century on his own home planet, Kairos is deaf to Giuliana's explanations.

"Signora, I know your Carlotta! If you will listen . . ."

But now, it seems Mamma is deaf. Dad's on video chat and he sounds totally p.o.'d. "Listen to me, Gwen! I'm worried she may not be there in time."

"What are you saying, Jerry? In time for what? The concert? Because I will stay here and wait. And believe you me, when she shows up, that girl is going to get a big piece of my mind!"

Dad harrumphs. "Right. Well, I'm here to say, that could be a really long time."

Mamma interrupts. "That's cryptic. What in the world are you talking about, Jerry?"

"Well, you know that crazy science fair project she was talking about—Leonardo da Vinci. Florence. Time machine."

I steel myself: Here it comes! The part where they banish me from the family—because of a little accidental shift of classified information onto my tablet, and the whole space-time continuum—like I could've known the top secret work going on in Operation Firenze!

"I didn't think Charley could actually breach our servers to tinker with this experimental stuff at work. We're talking the highest level of security clearance, Gwen! If she actually was able to unlock the code to the Qualia Rosetta . . . daughter or no, I'm going to have to report this."

I wanna say that I'm okay, and nothing catastrophic has happened. But they can't hear me, and, now, Jerry's just winding up.

"Our daughter may be smart, but even she could not have broken the code to a top secret government program without some high-level assistance," Mom insists. "There's gotta be some other explanation."

"You don't think her friend Billy—?"

Kairos is nodding his head like a crazy man, but Mamma's too wrapped up in what Dad's suggesting to pay him any mind.

Next to me, Billy freezes up when he hears his name. "Charley? The note I left for your dad—I didn't give away your secret. About breaking into your dad's classified stuff. I promise!"

"Too late now," I sigh.

"Not to mention what's posted on her Facebook," Dad continues. "A selfie of two kids dressed in costume, tagged "Carnevale, Firenze." Girl who could be right out of a Renaissance painting. One of those tight caps covering her head. Long dress with pleats around the neckline. So I posted a note on Charley's wall for whoever wrote this to contact me."

But Mamma's apparently still puzzling over the hacked operations. "Hmm, well. If Billy is in on this . . . Nice kid, but a little too quiet. I suspect he might know something about this."

Billy bows his head lower.

"Jerry, if the average hacker were to find the how-to for time travel among all the levels of classification, aren't there layers of encryption? And aren't the codes locked in a secure vault in your office?" Mamma pauses, lost in the chain of logic.

In the background, the orchestra is tuning up. I can hear the concertmaster shout, "Visitors and guests must leave. Musicians—places, please!"

Kairos motions to Giuliana to follow him out. "Gwen, I will come backstage to check on you during the intermezzo."

Mom barely nods at her friend.

But I've never heard Dad so angry. "You know, Gwen, my job might be on the line here."

"I know, Jerry. I've contacted the authorities with Charley's description on this end to put out an all-points bulletin, in case she somehow has managed to travel here, to Florence. Though I can't really imagine how."

She pauses. "Keep trying on your side, okay? And check out this Lex kid, too, okay? Charley seems to have developed a crush on him."

"Lex? And how do you expect me to find him?"

"Oh, you were fourteen once, Jerry. I bet if you put your mind to it, you could track down a frisky teenage boy without too much difficulty. Check Charley's Facebook again, for God's sake."

The orchestra is tuning up. Then I hear the opening strains of our song, Mamma's and mine.

"*Ciao, mio cuore. Pronto!* I feel like we're hot on her trail."

I am brought back to my Renaissance reality by a now-familiar little voice. "We must make haste!" insists Carolina, pulling me along and into a run. I hand the tablet back to Lex to stow in his backpack.

"It is time to don our masks for *il ballo in maschera!*" Carolina calls out.

It seems we have no choice but to follow: Carolina is in command.

XIV.
PRELUDE TO A MARDI GRAS BALL

We run posthaste back to Lorenzo's palace. The grand foyer is empty except for a few servants carrying heaping silver platters for a sumptuous Carnevale feast. A beaming Elisabetta rushes out to greet us. Wearing the costume of a shepherdess, Bethy II could've stepped right out of a Botticelli painting.

Not to be rude, I start with some quick introductions. "Bethy, these are my friends, Billy and—" She runs right past Billy and his upraised palm. Rude.

"You are Lex, no? *Mio cuore!*" She wraps him in a warm Florentine embrace.

"My, oh my!" Lex exclaims. "And where did you come from, beautiful?"

If I were to tell you there were sparks, it would be an understatement.

Elisabetta's getup clearly adds to her allure. While it's not quite the "sexy witch" costume I've seen some of the high school girls wearing on Halloween, it is still rather, shall I say, revealing.

I frown. "Bethy, is Leonardo here?"

Carolina chimes in. "Their masks, Elisabetta! Your friends must not be recognized! Savonarola and the Weepers must not find them here."

The Weepers are like Fra Savonarola's cheering squad, but way noisier. If there were an alt-media outlet here, it would be the wailing group of followers that amplifies the Franciscan brother's messages warning against the evils of art, books, beauty, and learning.

Carolina's warning distracts Bethy enough to relax her chokehold on Lex. She gets all defensive.

"Carolina, *mia madre e una Piagnoni*—a Weeper—and my aunt Viola too. I do not believe Savonarola would carry out his edicts to hunt down witches and heretics here, no matter what Kairos says."

And then, considering who she's sounding off to, Bethy relents. "*Come per te*, Carolina, you must go! You know *Magnifico* frowns upon children at the feasts!"

Carolina's lip begins to quiver, and for a moment I fear she might make a scene. "I won't go," she says, stomping her feet. "I am old enough! Besides, Carlotta needs my help."

"Carolina, don't be stupid. You must run home before I get in trouble for your appearance here!"

And on deeper inspection, Bethy notices that, under Billy's jacket, I am still soaking.

"Carlotta, come with me and we will fit you in a costume. Come, everyone. It is time to don the masks."

We all run down to the room with *La Primavera*, once again perfectly hung and seeming none the worse for wear.

Bethy checks behind the sofa and pulls out a large, carved wooden chest with a heavy lid. Lex chivalrously runs over to help her.

Kairos comes in at that moment. "Presto! The perfect disguise for Billy!" He pulls out checkered pants and a Harlequin mask.

"Radical, dude." Lex whistles in approval and Bethy appears once again to be distracted.

I hold out my hand expectantly. "Ahem. My costume?"

Bethy II, acting all meek and helpless, turns back to peer at Lex before she takes my hand. "Do not forget me, Lex-y." She runs me down

the hall to the same water closet where I was hiding out earlier in the day, trying to make sense of this unreal world.

"For you, Carlotta: You will be Columbina." Bethy smooths out the ragged-looking dress that will be my new disguise.

Columbine. I remember seeing an old-fashioned Punch and Judy puppet show at the Maryland Renaissance Festival once. In old Italian commedia dell'arte she was a servant girl, dressed in rags, but often the smartest character in the play. Her name means "little dove." So I'm guessing I have to play the part.

I slip off my wet clothes and ball them up in a corner, where I suddenly spy, glinting out of the shadows, a golden compass. Huh? How did . . . ? But I thought . . . ? So first the compass and maquette disappear from my backpack, and now the compass shows up here. I have a sneaking suspicion Kairos is behind this magic act, making objects appear and disappear, just like his own mysterious comings and goings.

"Carlotta," Bethy scolds, "why did you not tell me that you and Bee-ly. . . he is your boyfriend?"

Why do people here keep saying things like that? "He is *not* my boyfriend, Bethy!"

With a disbelieving glance, she slips the robe over my head. Tying on the mask, I peer into the glass and stare. No more Charley. My transformation from a twenty-first century teen into a Renaissance girl is complete.

Bethy pulls me by the hand as we run back down the hallway to meet up with the boys. "We must not be late, Carlotta!" I squint to see, but my mask keeps slipping down.

"Columbina, is that you?" shouts the now-masked Harlequin, a.k.a. Billy. He's wearing the diamond-checkered costume of the servant-clown who plays Columbine's male alter ego. The main giveaway is his stupid duffle, strapped over his shoulder. Which he'd better not lose, because it's got my violin in it!

Apparently liberated by his disguise, Billy grabs me by the hands and starts dancing me in a circle. Without warning, he puts his arms around me in a bear hug, and I feel a tingling down my spine.

Kairos whistles, breaking up the moment. "Now, wait until you see my perfect disguise!" He knocks on the wall to find the secret panel door, where I had been hiding earlier, and slips inside.

Bethy bends back over the costume chest. "And now, Lexy. You will be the *bandito* who steals my sheep!"

She pulls out a crook, a rough calfskin vest, and some ragged pants, which Lex tugs over his clothes. Then Bethy ties a black bandit mask over his face, touching Lex's cheek. "It is a crime that we must conceal this fair face."

Lex, adjusting the mask around his eyes, finds Bethy's hand over his. He practically stumbles over his own feet, stepping accidentally on hers; they embrace to avoid falling.

The whole thing looks ridiculous. I'm about to start my fake laugh when Kairos bursts back into the room, brandishing a baseball glove and ball, interrupting the awkward embrace between Lex and Bethy. He's sporting a Washington Nationals uniform and Billy's cap.

Lex laughs and slaps him on the back. "Put 'er there, man," he says, doing a fist bump. "I'll give you a little fielding practice later!"

"I am, how you say—a Washington National in de' Medici's court!"

"Who would ever even imagine . . ." Billy steps back and takes in the sight—five teens out of time. "Group photo!" he shouts, whipping out his old flip phone as Lex gathers us into a huddle under his broad arms—me on one side, Bethy II on the other, and bookended by Billy and Kairos.

"No, here, wait!" I dig into Lex's backpack, remembering the replacement tablet. "Let's use this tablet. Say *formaggio!*" Bethy II, unfamiliar with the expression, not to mention having one's photograph taken, shapes her mouth in an O.

We huddle close together. Lex stretches his long arm out far enough to fit us all into the picture. Masks all around, no one but us will know who's who in this selfie.

I take the tablet to show Bethy her image. "*Ancora!*" she exclaims. "It is, *como si dice,* Carlotta? Amazeballs!"

I giggle at her amazement. "It's just a picture, Elisabetta!" I tease.

Kairos, suddenly serious, starts barking out instructions. "For you girls"—he points to me and Bethy—"there is no time to lose. The masked ball is beginning. It's the only opportunity for you to come out in the open, Carlotta, and it is there we will find the maestro."

"Need to do one thing real quick," Lex interrupts, grabbing the tablet back from me. "Posting this picture to—"

I jump in. "No! Lex, no one gets to see this picture outside of us. 'Cause where you gonna send it—home to Beth? Like she's gonna help!"

I feel a slight pang. After all I've seen and experienced in the last day, it seems I was wrong to judge my twenty-first century best friend.

But it's too late. He's posted it to Instagram: #timetraveler #Carnival #Italianstyle #pals #history.

I grab the tablet out of his hands, praying that status updates are blocked on government-issue devices or, at least that in the future, my BFF Beth won't recognize me.

But such hope is futile. 'Cause like magic, the tablet video chat app opens.

There's Bethy the First texting and checking her Instagram. "Hell's bells!" I exclaim. "This is perfect. Perfectly awful."

Billy looks startled. I never cuss. Not that it's a religion with me or anything, I just love words and would rather utilize more descriptive than coarse ones.

Beth is sprawled on top of her bed. She swings her legs over to scrutinize Lex's status update.

"What the heck? Is this a joke, like trick or treat? That girl in the middle with the mask sliding off her face and the wild hair. If I didn't know better, I'd think it's Charley!"

"Double hell," I say, pushing my mask back up.

Bethy I moves in closer, pinching the picture wider. For a minute, it looks like there's a ghost of recognition on her face. Then she frowns. "Naw, that can't be Charley. Her dad posted an update on her Facebook page; like, they're running all over creation looking for her."

Kairos leans over me, whispering, "We must go, Carlotta. *Andiamo!*"

"Wait! I just need to hear what she's saying."

Bethy II scoots in to get a closer look. "*È quella la tua Elisabetta, Carlotta?*"

"Yes, my other Elizabeth. My one and only former best friend."

Billy's growing impatient. "Charley, we need to get out there and find Leo. He's the only one who can rescramble the time code. It's our best chance."

I'm torn between saving my life and seeing what Bethy I's gonna do about it.

"*Bene. Andiamo!*" I sigh, and Billy leads me by the arm to . . . wherever it is Kairos is taking us. But I can't take my eyes off the screen. Lex, too, seems engrossed in the home front. He matches my stride so we can check it out together.

"This is too weird," says Beth I. "I'm sure Lex posted this as a hoax. I mean, her parents think she hitched a plane to Florence to see her mom. How could Lex and Charley be together? And why would anybody in Italy be wearing a Nats uniform! Or . . . could Lex have totally betrayed me? No, he wouldn't. How could he?"

Beth's trying to sound matter-of-fact, even though, where anything "Lex" is concerned, I know she's totally gaga.

"Typical Beth. Totally thinking about herself."

"I dunno, Charley. For now, though, we need to keep moving."

Lex—the Lex at my side at this moment—stares directly back at the screen, repeating like it's a mantra, "*Time travel works. Time travel works. Time travel works.*"

Beth heaves a dramatic sigh. "Maybe I should alert Mr. Morton. After his 911 update on Facebook and all." I see her punching numbers on her phone.

Which apparently rings directly to voicemail. "Hi, Mr. M. I saw Charley's Instagram. Lex posted a video like he's at a costume ball! And Billy . . . anyways, I don't know where Charley is. But it's gonna be okay. Don't ask me how, but we're gonna get her home, 'k? Oh, and yeah, it's me, Beth." And she hangs up.

"Yeah, like she's really doing something to make that happen." I sigh.

Still, it's a start.

But I'm losing her virtual voice in the growing din around us. We're close to the palace ballroom now. There's an orchestra playing—badly, in my personal judgment—and, like, a million people in costume. Beautiful courtesans flirting their way from group to group. Imposing men in uniform standing sentinel—the royal guard? I wonder if Viola is one of them. Were women allowed in *Magnifico's* official forces? Servants streaming in and out with wine, mead, and steaming dishes. A few of these servants look familiar—is this what Signora Vincenzo would be doing?

As the music plays—Lorenzo de' Medici's own compositions, no doubt—couples stream to the dance floor, where they weave and whirl with grace across the floor in stately step, not unlike the courtly bow I have not yet perfected. Even among the courtiers, I spy a few not-so-courteous pinches and clutches as these dancers promenade, bow close, then part, spin, and turn to the next partner.

XV.
THE MAIN EVENT

No matter what, I'm not dancing. I'd either twist my ankle again or fall flat on my face. Besides, too much attention right now would probably not be such a hot idea. I stand by the side of the orchestra platform, tapping my good toe in time.

I wish I could tune them up—their instruments are seriously out of register. Imagine my surprise when I see it is none other than Leonardo da Vinci himself who leads them, conducting expressively with both hands. He strums the lute in interludes, as the various wind instruments, horns, and drummers bang away. They sound like a Renaissance garage band. Without the garage. There's a harp and several giant viola-like instruments. But no violins!

Billy startles me by coming up from behind. "Ew! Sounds like birds in a catfight. You play so much better! Why don't you show 'em how it's done, Charley?"

He's about to drop the duffel to the ground; I dive to save my dear instrument from impact.

"Really?" Carefully, I turn and move into a corner where I'm less likely to be noticed. I open the duffle and gently lift my violin out of the bag. Caressing my old friend, my fingers get itchy. I untie my mask—the thing keeps slipping off. Luckily, Billy has the presence of mind to find a scarf to arrange strategically over my hair and forehead, which also keeps Translator under wraps, literally! I adjust it above my eyes and pull it tighter—the wool is scratchy and I'm nervous that I'll be playing blind.

I place the instrument under my chin. That smooth wood feels familiar and reminds me of home. Which reminds me of Mamma.

Billy hands me the bow from his bag. My hands are shaking.

"Maybe this isn't such a great idea, Billy," I say shakily.

"Aw, Charley, c'mon." He seems so insistent. "What other violinist will ever have the chance to say she's played live with a Renaissance orchestra under the lead of Maestro Leonardo himself!"

Boy genius has a point. There will never in history be such a moment again. I quietly bow a few notes on my instrument, wondering how to tune it to match the orchestra. And then, legs feeling like rubber, I take a few steps toward the bandstand.

Leonardo, spying me out of the corner of his eye, nods to the orchestra, which falls silent. Between my strange getup and my even stranger instrument, all eyes are on me.

I'm scared half to death, but what have I got to lose? They've already decided I'm a witch. I'm playing for time!

I pluck out the basic tune for "Leo" amid new stares from the party-goers until Leonardo nods and smiles, and lifts his hand to get the orchestra to join in. They join in enthusiastically behind me, giving me more confidence.

Leonardo steps over to stand beside me. I pick up the tempo and grin, as the revelers resume their dancing.

Which does nothing to stop nearby bystanders from whispering and clucking behind their masks, or from madly waving ostrich-feather fans: "Scandalous!" "Who is this stranger?" "What is this she plays?" "Is she one of Magnifico's protégées, or his mistress?"

I don't care! My violin is sacred. Each time I draw the bow across its strings, the music transports me to another world—my own.

At song's end, Leonardo nods to me, to the musicians, and to the crowd. An expectant hush falls over the room, as it appears he is about to speak.

"*Signore e signori*," he intones. "I show you my newest improvement on the traditional lute." He holds up his lute for all to see. "I call it . . . er, it is called . . ."

"The violin!" I blurt out as he falters. And immediately regret it. I wonder if I haven't, again, changed some timeline for an instrument that isn't known to have been invented for another half century or so.

"*Si*," Leonardo affirms. "Violin. Rather like the viola da gamba, but smaller, and played under the chin." He nods at me to play, and listens with everyone looking on.

I feel naked with embarrassment, but as it seems I am playing some new instrument designed and built by Leonardo, how can I not demonstrate?

"Most beautiful, do you all not think? Now, since music be the wellspring of dance, we shall play on!"

He closes his eyes and joins in on his own instrument. Together, we improvise, and by the movement of his body, I can tell that he, too, is transported by the music. He's in the zone.

How can this be! I think wondrously. Me, playing a duet with Leonardo da Vinci on an instrument that bends the timeline!

He signals to the orchestra to join in.

On an impulse, I stop playing for a moment. What a thrill; this ragtag group on stage with their badly tuned instruments is playing my song! So what if their instruments aren't perfectly tuned?

And you know what's weird? Right then, I imagine I am hearing an entire string section of an orchestra building my song layer upon layer, harmony upon harmony. A much fuller sound. Amazing what the mind fills in to make a picture whole.

Leonardo then signals to me, and under his upraised baton, the ragtag band drops out, and it's me playing solo. Until . . . it sounds as though another violin has joined in. It's like I can hear Mamma playing, at least in my imagination. Our duet.

Suddenly, the other violin stops. Then I stop. She starts again. Is it really her? My violin, then hers, over and over. We're trading stanzas. Is that possible?

I nod to Billy. *"Record us,"* I mouth. If what I'm hearing is actually happening, this would be proof certain: Music can echo across centuries.

I imagine someone, somewhere, someday posting this on YouTube, where it gets millions of page views. That would make me so happy. "Breaking news: #Mother #daughter #duet. Musical bond transcends time."

I would show this to my future little brother or sister, and perhaps it would inspire them to make music too.

For now that day is far, far, far in the future.

I let go of my reverie at the sound of clapping. I open my eyes to look as the din gets louder. They are clapping for me!

Now everyone seems swept away by the sound. Dancers are whirling around us, and partygoers gossiping behind their fans, but even as these masqueraders engage in their familiar celebration, *their* world is changing forever—for all time—because of *us*.

A humbling thought.

Billy's jumping around, taping us and attracting a little too much attention. Elisabetta sashays around him, obviously wanting to move her feet. She pulls Billy away and over to the dance floor.

I give him the hairy eyeball for abandoning his taping duties. More to the point, I feel a pang. He's not a bad dancer, Billy.

I don't want to dance. But I do want him to dance with me!

They haven't gone far when Lex taps Billy on the shoulder, cutting in. Billy gets his feet tangled up in Elisabetta's long shepherdess dress, sending her tumbling.

They've created a scene on the dance floor, and Billy looks helpless. Lex helps Bethy II to her feet and, clinging tightly to his arm, Bethy casts a wink in my direction. With a motion, she gets Billy untangled and pushes him toward the orchestra platform, whence he crashes into the percussion section. Cymbals crash.

"Oops, um, well, er . . . sorry everybody. I mean, *prego*," he stammers. Billy's mask is askew and his face is flushing. He's out there: no artifice. Just klutzy, geeky, endearing Billy.

He's making me crazy!

We've now captured the attention of everyone in the room. Embarrassed, I curtsy to Leonardo and the other players, set down my instrument, and step away from the bandstand.

Billy slinks over to his duffel and starts fiddling with the Operation Firenze tablet in full view!

This starts even more buzz.

I pronto pull him away somewhere I hope is less conspicuous, even as the crowd goes wild.

"Whoa, Billy. Are you trying to get their attention?"

"Charley, no, I just need to listen to what I recorded."

"You were recording all that time?"

He looks at me like, duh, of course I wouldn't abandon my duty. "What I heard, or think I heard . . . This starts out being your playing with this orchestra, then, when you get to the second verse—"

"It's not like pop music, Billy. There aren't verses!"

He stomps his foot. "Just shut up a minute, Charley, why don't you. Listen!"

He winds the recording back, and I press Translator against my ears to muffle all the other sounds. A parade of servants is now bringing more food out, and people are exclaiming at the feast of feasts and shuffling back to the tables lining the rest of the hall to eat yet another course.

"Okay, this is the first part. Tell me what you're hearing."

First, it sounds like what was playing in this ballroom, the dissonant sounds of the ragtag orchestra I was just playing with. But as the tempo picks up, so does the musicianship.

Holding my breath, I listen to strains of what could only be the National Symphony's full orchestration of "Leo." At the appointed moment comes the violin solo (Mamma, is it you?!), and the final crescendo, with a crash of cymbals and drums.

I let out my breath. "It's got to be my mom and the symphony, Billy. Play it again." I hold my ears to listen more intently.

"Omigod! We can test out the theory that sound waves might travel across time. I wouldn't have guessed we could transmit actual recognizable music! What if maybe I could play something back to her so she'd know it was me?"

At that moment, one of the servants steps in between me and Billy, holding a tray with something that smells delicious. "Hey!" I shout hangrily. "Look where you're going!"

The servant turns with a nod and a blink, and who should it be, but Carolina! "Well, you little imp! Who said you could stay?"

But before I can hear her reply, Billy is pulling me by the arm. "No time for chitchat, Charley. Here, take your instrument."

At the same time, Billy grabs the office tablet. He pulls me into a little antechamber off the ballroom. No one here but us.

"Okay, now—if you want to try it," urges my geeky friend, moving closer to record me playing.

Ignoring the orchestra, which has loudly begun to play Lorenzo de'

Medici's Carnevale music just outside our hideaway, I tuck my violin under my chin and begin playing snippets of the overture to *The Magic Flute*. That's the Mozart piece I was practicing at home when all was mostly right with the world—and before I upended the normal course of human events to bend time. I know the NSO has *The Magic Flute* on the Florence program—which is why I was trying to learn it in the first place, to keep up with Mamma and make her proud.

After several measures I stop and hear the unmistakable modern-day echo. Crazier still, the players here don't seem to notice. I guess that's a good thing; after all, Mozart won't be born for another two centuries or more.

But what is time, after all, when I can see the whole of history playing out from here? So I'm no longer surprised to see the video chat open on the tablet.

Same room, same palace, same music. Different orchestra. And different century. They have a projection screen where the National Symphony is performing. It must be so the members in the back of the orchestra can see the conductor in real time, no matter what other obstructions there may be. Technology changes everything.

And there's Mamma! Gwen taps her feet nervously; another solo should be coming up. She must be anxious: She drops a page of music off the stand and misses a few bars. Luckily, the rest of the orchestra can cover the lapse.

I pick out the missing violin stanzas at the same time.

As she picks up the pages and rifles quickly through the score, she appears distracted. I continue to play the notes—missing one or two on purpose, so she'll know it's me. And then, like magic, she's got it; she's echoing me, note for note.

We are only measured notes and heartbeats apart.

"My God, could I be hearing . . . ?" she whispers.

There's a place in the score where the first violinist has a sixteen-measure rest, and it's at that moment when Mamma is able to look off-stage, searching for me where I am not. She looks back up at the screen to see the conductor and the rest of the orchestra, and there I am—or here I am there? There I will be? It's so surreal.

The point is, for that one moment, we see each other in unison through the curtain of time. And as Billy's been recording her, Mamma surreptitiously pulls her phone from the music stand and aims at the screen where she sees . . . me?

We may, in fact, be recording the earliest multi-century, multi-location livestream duet recording in music history. At both ends!

Perhaps inspirited by having seen me, Mamma attacks her next solo. The crowd erupts in spontaneous applause, though the piece is not yet over. Realizing where she is, she nods graciously.

As the rest of the orchestra plunges into the next movement, she covertly pulls out her phone again, this time, I am guessing, to text my dad the video.

Billy flashes the U.S. government–issued tablet in front of me to show me Mamma's text to Dad. DON'T ASK HOW BUT LOCATED CHARLEY & FRIENDS. SHE'S OKAY. *BRAVISSIMA!*

Then, without waiting for Dad's response, she joyously plays on.

XVI.
CHAOS THEORY

Back in time, though, all is pandemonium.
Diners have overstuffed their faces with food and wine, and enough drinking has gone on that the joviality in the crowd is turning into irritation. All this musical stopping and starting, my mysterious instrument, Billy crashing into the cymbals—adding up to general suspicion among the crowd. Even the guards seem to be getting restless. They have been drinking and carousing right along with the rest of the guests, but they have their eyes on us. On me.

Time to blend in. I stow the violin gingerly in Billy's sack, seize him by the shoulders, and pull poor, clueless Billy back onto the dance floor. We practice our Renaissance bows, trying to copy the dancers around us, me wincing at every wrong twist and turn of my ankle. Lex and Bethy II are similarly engaged.

"You guys!" I whisper just loud enough for them to hear. "It's gonna be okay! I heard my mom playing out of time! She can hear us!"

Billy looks unconvinced. "Humph. I don't know what good that will do, really. Not until we get to talk to Leo."

I frown. "I've got to get home, Billy. Don't you get it?"

"I know, Charley. I want to go home too. But, as long as we're here . . . dance with me?"

Billy bows low before me. I do my practiced bow in reply.

"Veloce, con spirito!" Without warning, Leo cues the musicians to bump up the tempo to a frenzy.

Billy and I lose the courtly steps and give it up to freestyling. Lex follows, and after watching a minute or two, Bethy II joins in joyously.

"Charley. I'm sorry. Sorry for everything," Lex shouts over the ruckus.

What does that mean, sorry? Is he sorry he kissed me? Sorry he sent me hurtling here? Sorry he followed me? Sorry that Bethy II is smitten?

But everything is changed. I glimpse over at masked Billy. He's dancing with abandon, looking silly, but having a blast.

"S'okay, Lex, I forgive you."

Our newfangled dance moves are raising more than a few eyebrows. Again, there's too much attention on us. A circle of young dancers assembles around us, clapping to this new Renaissance rock 'n' roll beat.

Kairos moves into our circle and invites all the younger people to join us. Before I know what's happening, he is forming a snake line around Leonardo, who, strumming his lute and wiggling Elvis-style, is, in one more domain, a star.

There's a mounting murmur from the crowd. The guardsmen hold their hands on the hilts of their swords. Is *Magnifico* among them? He certainly wouldn't allow a bunch of teens to hijack his celebration.

On the other hand, it is Mardi Gras, that *"laissez les bons temps rouler"* time of year. Guests are laughing, yelling, singing, and spilling wine all over the marble floors and each other. The women are shrieking—in delight or fear, I can't decide. Many of their men somehow look like they're begging for a fight.

"I don't know about you guys," Lex interjects, "but this party looks about to erupt. And we're not talking fun flash mob, either."

As chaos breaks out and the orchestra disassembles, Leonardo signals in our direction.

"Let's go!" Kairos hurries us to another massive hall nearby—one that has been prepared with long banquet tables and even more jugs of wine and heaping serving trays.

I have to say that it all smells heavenly to a girl who hasn't eaten in many lifetimes. I grab bunches of fat purple grapes—the only food that looks acceptable to eat without utensils here—and start stuffing them into my mouth. Biting down on the smooth, soft skins releases the succulent sweetness inside. The juice drools down my chin.

Leonardo seems fired up with inspiration. He clears away several places from the table with arcing sweeps of his long painter's arms to make room to diagram whatever plans he's dreamed up. He wields his charcoal like a conductor's baton, waving it in the air to think, then sketching out his thoughts on the white cloth covering the table. I'm pretty sure whoever ends up sitting here's gonna think that Lorenzo de' Medici has gone out of his mind with table word-art decorations.

"The inverse of the golden ratio, which we use in music, art, and across the field of life to describe perfect proportion . . ." Leo begins. Then he sets down this formula: $\varphi = b/a = a/b + a$.

He breaks the charcoal, offering me half, but Billy immediately grabs it out of my hands and starts scribbling his own equations. I bend over Billy's shoulder to double-check him.

"This, we would understand, is the Qualia Rosetta," Billy says. I half think to stop him; our knowing so much about the work behind Operation Firenze is evidence that could be used against us.

But no one else seems to be paying Billy any mind.

"You may think: The soul is composed of harmony," Leonardo muses. "Music is dependent upon hearing but, unlike painting, fades away as soon as it is born. Or does it? After all, do we not say that music transports us?"

"It certainly transported me!" I comment woefully. "Right to Mamma!"

Kairos gives me a nervous look. Funny reaction, coming from someone who I saw with Mamma, in person, just moments ago.

"Maestro, it is more than music that has carried us all to this point," I observe.

Billy steps back from the table, satisfied enough with his doodles to explain them. "The space-time formula looks like a four-dimensional manifold, like a place in time projected on a flat map of the Earth that curves back and around itself to form a globe. What's beyond the globe? We can only imagine."

"Traveling to the past is actually harder, because it requires one to exceed the speed of light," I interject.

Billy looks admiringly at me. "Just so, Charley. Once we don't have to account for the reversal of motion in the positron, or the faster-than-light-speed Higgs Boson, traveling forward in time looks to be a snap. It just takes energy. Lots and lots of energy!"

I see where he's taking this idea. "We're a long time from being able to prove it here, but splitting an atom releases enough energy to provide electricity to light up a city."

"Yeah, or blow it up—and us with it!" Lex interjects gloomily.

Leonardo is studying Billy's equation thoughtfully. "Since your atom won't be successfully split for another half a millennium, we must harness existing forces around us."

Kairos, the dude who's repeatedly ridden the waves of time, chimes in. "There is a powerful-enough force, like an ocean wave. The moon governs waves, tides, and the Earth below. But I have not understood before a way to allow anyone to ride them at will without . . . I cannot describe this in a way that would serve you at present—or even quite yet in Carlotta's time—without changing the trajectory of discovery in ways not salubrious to your future."

"Yeah, what he says," Lex affirms, as if that explains anything.

Of course, I have a million questions. "So, you're saying that one day we will devise a higher form of mathematics to describe forces beyond—"

Leonardo, impatient, chimes in. "Even if one were able to amass, in one point—a singularity, you'd call it?—the force of all the waves in the sea, I do not see how this would be enough to push you forward across centuries."

"And we are not all that clear about mapping the destination with any accuracy!" I point out.

"If we could create a vortex with sufficient energy . . . ," Leonardo muses.

I jump in excitedly. "In the modern day, they've created this massive gyrating machine under the earth—a frictionless tunnel that generates enough force to amp up to light speed. The CERN lab. You remember, we talked about this earlier this afternoon. Some cosmologists think there might be wormholes, Maestro Leonardo—shortcuts to new dimensions and other universes."

I model an inchworm with my finger crawling across the table and poking it through the cracks to demonstrate. Bethy makes a face.

"They think these are holes, or tunnels, in the fabric of space-time. Remember Einstein? Of course, even if we were to find such a thing from here, which is doubtful, it's less than guaranteed to bring us back to the right universe!"

"But there is only one universe where time shoots straight as an arrow in a forward direction!" Leonardo says in astonishment. "And you are saying that, in your day, they have found multiple universes with alternate entries?"

Billy nods. "The math does seem to bear out that possibility."

Leonardo's eyes light up and his whole demeanor changes. "Would that I could see such a marvel!"

I'm thinking Michelangelo's Sistine ceiling might be a fair representation, what with God out in the heavens reaching in to touch Adam, in our universe. But painting on that won't start for at least ten more years.

Another not yet.

Meanwhile, Leonardo is so in the moment, wormholes and universes before him. "From your cosmology, you're saying there's no sure way, at this point, to find a way to the right, how do you say—'wormhole'?—to get you home?" He inches his own finger in the air.

Bethy giggles. Seeing her all fidgety now, I get that not everyone would find this a compelling conversation. But to me, this is the stuff of genius!

At all these revelations, Lex looks glum. "Let's just find a roadmap then. You know, like take a left at the second star, merge into the passing lane, and take the underpass into Wherever-land," he says sarcastically.

Billy ignores this. "What about rocket power?"

"Blasting off Earth today and returning to an Earth of the future? Hah! Like that's gonna work," Lex concludes.

Kairos is pacing. "Don't get your pantaloons in a knot," he interjects, pinpointing the Renaissance origins of a modern-day cliché about twisted knickers. "We have the key—the maestro's Qualia Rosetta. That is the formula inside your golden compass that will unlock the portal to your future. The power and potential will be unlocked at precisely the moment required."

"Qualia Rosetta," Leonardo repeats. "A key to the subjective experience of time."

Lex is thinking. "You mean, like, when you're up at bat, the ball's flying at you faster than you have time to think, but, still, you hit just that sweet spot to connect with the ball and drive that baby over the fence? When you're so in the zone you don't even know that you've just hit the home run of your life?!"

"Yeah. Like that, Lex," I say. For myself, I have to say, I am not convinced that anyone's being in the zone gets us anywhere.

But our back-and-forth seems to have sparked something in Leonardo; he's started sketching again.

"The idea of flight into orbit—this intrigues me!" Leonardo exclaims. "A ship that has the aerodynamic design to break free of the constraints of the Earth and to circle the globe at your light speed. Does Ser *Eye-n-stey-n* conclude this would be possible, in fact?"

He shows us his doodles. "Look here, this needs be streamlined, with fins for stability for constant acceleration. Then how to create enough of

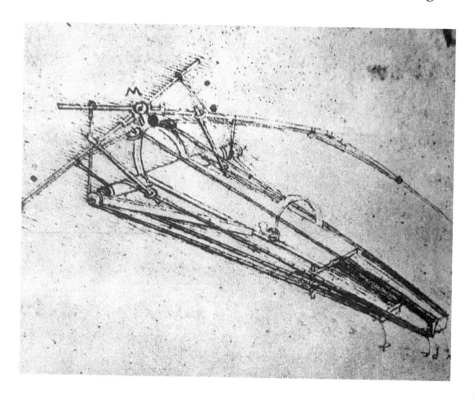

a heat shield that the ship would not be overheated by friction?"

"Hate to break it to you, maestro, but we have no rocket fuel," I inform him. "And Einstein says we can't travel as fast as light."

"But you have, in fact, achieved this," Leo says, looking at the three of us.

"We'd need a boatload of gunpowder, for sure!" Billy adds, seemingly willing to argue with Einstein's proof.

"Cannon power!" Leonardo exclaims. "My tri-barreled cannons in an array, with a single fuse to ignite these."

"Um-hmm." I am unconvinced. I want to get back to the facts. Mamma and I seemed to open a portal to each other simply by playing in time. "And the music? Perhaps this is another frequency of communication—always present but waiting for something—or someone—to receive it. Like radio signals."

"*Si*. This is possible. Musical notes rise and fall according to the vibration of energies created by the instruments, whether through blowing, strumming, or the plucking of strings." Leonardo gets it instinctively. There's something to that experience of music.

I nod. "I think those variations of energies create the harmonies and colors of the universe. They should also be able to transport us, no?"

I can see Billy's itching to get moving. "Brilliant, man. Every object in the universe has its music. Including us. We can totally make this work."

Lex brings us back to reality. "So, guys, here's the deal: Charley's in danger. And me and Billy aren't far behind. Too much talk, not enough action here—we gotta go!"

That's when I notice the sound of heavy boots tromping outside our hall. I scan the edges of the room and feel the tension shift: Lorenzo's sentries, armed with swords and daggers, have moved to places outside this banquet room.

Leonardo is still preoccupied with the talk about energy. "Here sound, here colors, here the character of every part of the universe concentrated to a point. At its essence, matter may change form, from waves to particles and back."

I'm trying to pull something from my admittedly exhausted memory. "Well, yes, I'd have to say, in my trip across time it was like waves and particles interacted and alternated to reshape my experience of time. So that's the qualia—the subjective experience. . . ."

Billy jumps in. "True. 'Cause my experience was more like an explosion than a wave!"

This gets me thinking again. "If we know sound can break the time barrier, what if we could create multiple sound waves of increasing intensity?" I hum out as low a musical note as I can reach, then start up the scale. Then Kairos and Leonardo—the first a tenor, the second having a basso profondo—chime in, sustaining the harmonies. I'd have to say we'd make an awesome a capella group!

Billy's not impressed. "So what's your point, Charley?"

Still humming, I start spinning like a top, arms spread wide, until, dizzy and out of breath, I fall to the ground.

Picking me up and forming a circle of hands with Billy, Kairos, and Lex, Leonardo dances us into a frenzy, humming and harmony all around, until we create a vibrational wall of sound.

This experiment leads to a dead end. "I dunno," I admit, and throw up my arms.

Leonardo tries to complete the puzzle. "Yes, I have observed that Earth rotates around *sol*, and not the other way around. If I understand . . . gravity is a force that acts with the Earth's rotation to keep us all from flying off the face of this planet and into space, no?"

I sit cross-legged on the ground and pat the floor to affirm how firmly we are planted, even though I don't feel at all rooted at the moment.

"So reversing the spin of the Earth," Leonardo continues, "while increasing acceleration, might reverse gravity and hence the flow of time."

Kairos looks aghast. "Surely, maestro, you do not suggest we reverse the spin of the Earth?!"

Sounds crazy, but no crazier than anything else that's happened in the past twenty-four hours.

"A new avenue for discovery!" Leonardo falls silent for a moment. "For you see, learning is the only thing the mind never exhausts, never fears, and never regrets."

"Yeah, yeah. All that's well and good, Leo." I'm feeling a new sense of urgency as we hear the sentries outside our ballroom doors begin barking out orders. "But for now, we've gotta get back to the future."

Leonardo sits down on a window ledge, fist under his chin, the epitome of the thinker. "Were we to find a shortcut—this wormhole of which science speaks? What forces can we harness that would permit us to overcome gravity?"

"We'd need to rig together all the energy sources in the present to find a way to reach the future. Wind, solar, music, cannon fire . . . and a fuse. Leo, is your tri-barreled cannon mobile? Er, like, maybe on wheels?"

"Even so, it would take the strength of ten men to transport it. Perhaps a better solution: Were we to create this 'mass energy' force at the Piazza della Signoria, there are already nine massive cannons in use as fortification. And that holier-than-thou Savonarola has heaped mountains of treasure there to set ablaze. Further amplification, perhaps, for this incendiary experiment?"

I flail my hands. "Oh, yes! Imagine nine tri-barreled cannons like thunder firing at once—KAPOW! A twenty-seven-cannon salute. With a strong enough blast coming out of them all at once, plus if we can mock up some kind of windmill . . . if there's wind, of course . . . then if we have a strong noonday sun like we had today, with amplification from the solar panel—where's my backpack?"

I dig out the solar panel and set up a dock for the contraband U.S. government–issued tablet that, if I'm guessing right, has some powerful apps that might include high-vibration speakers.

There's a glint in Leonardo's eye as he taps those long artist fingers together in a rascally fashion.

Kairos looks concerned—like I've come unhinged. "Carlotta, I warn you: You are playing with fire. An explosion in the center of Florence could spark panic. And your wormhole: We must make sure that the spiral pulls you into the future. A turn in the wrong direction could send you even farther into history."

"I don't care what you say. Don't you see? I have to get home. Mamma needs me!"

XVII.
Let Them Burn!

The natives are restless. There seems to be a growing mob scene outside our room, stomping and clapping, with calls for Leonardo and his musicians and "that girl"—*quella ragazza*, a.k.a. me. The guards surely have drawn their swords against the threat of violence.

We cannot stay in the palazzo.

Leonardo leads us outside, where things get worse. Seems the *Piagnoni*—those fanatical Weepers who lead the rallies in Florence against knowledge, truth, and beauty—have learned of the "wicked" dancing, music, and mayhem breaking out inside the palace walls. They are "crying" in protest. Sounds to me more like high-pitched whining.

Standing on a platform beside one of the large pyramids of books, furs, wigs, paintings—tinder for the infamous bonfire of the vanities—is none other than Fra Girolamo Savonarola.

"There he is: the infamous Savonarola!" I poke Billy, who strains for a look.

The crowd is pressing against the gates, torches ablaze, like a mob threatening to storm the castle.

From a hilltop somewhere above the crowd rises a shrill voice. "Elisabetta! Kairos! *Tcharr-li!*"

"Carolina!" But I cannot make out her little face in the night's dappling of light and darkness cast by flaming torches.

Savonarola commands the silence of the Weepers. He is set to deliver one of his famous sermons. I can't take my eyes off this ghoul-faced man. Nor can I understand how he can stir grown men and women to weeping with his words.

"Oh, Florence! Many secrets are locked up here which cannot come out, especially because you would not believe them!"

"What is this?" With an air of command, Lorenzo de' Medici emerges into the crowd. "Who are these rabble-rousers who seek to destroy my festival?"

He runs up the steps to the platform, where his tall frame towers over Savonarola. "Fra Savonarola again stirs discontent. Has the pious priest not been warned?"

The guardsmen wave stanchions and swords, pushing their way through the wall of people to clear a path through the assembly for Lorenzo.

Leonardo hurries us all to a dim corner beyond the crowd.

I need to remain invisible, hidden in the shadows. But I am dying of curiosity. Like, here is history in the making, and we are eyewitnesses!

So when Savonarola speaks again, I climb on a little stone wall for a better view. There must be a weird trick of the sound bouncing off the palace walls: It sounds like Savonarola is directing his venom directly at Lorenzo, and Lorenzo alone.

"I warned you that you would see much evil and many tribulations. Now you have seen it, and see the troubles beginning, and the start of what I told you, and cannot deny it."

Lorenzo looks annoyed. "What nonsense you speak. My people need gaiety in their lives. Let them enjoy this feast before the fasting of Lent."

Savonarola sneers. "There is rot in the House of Medici that spreads throughout Florence."

The crowd falls preternaturally silent, as if straining not to miss a word.

Rot. Is he talking about me, or the so-called "vanities" he's ready to burn in the square? My heart is pounding so hard, I can hear it ring in my ears.

"*Tcharr-li!*" I hear Carolina singing out my name, and I want to hush her. 'Cause I don't think it's my imagination when I hear the crowd taking up the chant: "*Tcharr-li. Tcharr-li. Tcharr-li.*"

Billy leans close and puts an arm over my shoulders and whispers, "I don't think they know what they're saying, Charley."

As the crowd amps up, Savonarola picks up a torch and throws down the challenge: "Let everyone confess and be purged of his sins. Understand what I have said to you: This is the fire, That is the water; now act!"

Lorenzo mobilizes his guards, who come ever nearer to where we're crouched. My knees may buckle at any moment.

"Lock him up," Lorenzo commands. His guards move forward toward Savonarola.

The crowd also starts pushing, but in our direction. Our backs are literally against the wall. A new chant goes up in the crowd. "Water! Fire! Act!"

In my fevered brain I try to decipher their call. Water and fire—these are the tortures the Inquisition used to destroy heretics, witches, and false prophets. Burning at the stake was not uncommon!

Then I notice the "vanities" and the blazing torches of the crowd. I can imagine feeling these flames licking my feet, my arms, my face. Scorching my wild hair. *Una strega!*

"Is it me they're calling a witch?" I ask. But the surge of people in our direction leaves no time to ponder this.

At that moment, a small figure emerges from the crowd and flies toward us. "*Tcharr–li*, run!" shouts Carolina, running headlong in front of the crowd.

Kairos snares her by the hood of her cape. "Carolina. Go home!"

"NO!" she shouts. "I have heard Signora Vincenzo and Viola saying '*la strega* must burn!' They have said this to Savonarola himself!"

"Who—who—?" I sputter into silence.

"I know a way out, *Tcharr-li!* You and your friends—you must go!"

As if there was any doubt, the pious priest's next words obliterate it.

"Heed my words! Look within! These strangers in your midst, children. Root them out! They bring harm to Florence."

I can't move. My feet have become glued to the ground and my head might explode. This is it: D-Day, H-Hour.

Leonardo grabs my arm. "There is no longer time for games. We must carefully finalize the plan for the ultimate weapon to jettison you forward. I think your *Eye-n-stey-n* would predict, this is the most difficult challenge!"

I look over to Billy. He confirms we are ready to make this happen.

"Billy, you've brought supplies, yes? The golden compass? And of course, Ser Leonardo, we are deeply indebted! And Kairos—"

Billy jumps in. "Guys, let's just do it! We will need cannon power and more. What else might boost our energy output to add velocity?"

I hesitate, looking around. "Wait—where's Lex? I swear he was just here!"

Carolina, who, like her brother, seems to know everyone's whereabouts at all times, pipes up, "He has run back in, *Tcharr-li.* Looking for Elisabetta!"

"Are you kidding? What. An. Idiot."

Bethy and Lex; where could they have gone? A memory gnaws at my gut: the magic of a kiss. And there was undoubtedly a chemical reaction between those two. The fire of such passion has already triggered the time machine once.

Could history repeat itself—but with Elisabetta in my place? I must pull myself together. The future depends on it. "Maestro, where have you set up the time machine?"

His finger lands on the sketch. "Here," he says. "Tomorrow. Parades. Fireworks over the Arno by the Ponte Vecchio. And the key—the golden compasses that were lately in your possession. Carlotta, you still have these, yes?"

I double check that the one I found in the water closet is still in my pocket and pull it out. "And the Horse and Rider maquette—I know the second compass was locked into that."

Without hesitation, Billy nods. "Yes, and I copied the geo-location. Think, Charley—can we catch a satellite echo to map our coordinates? We'd pinpoint Takoma Park, Maryland, as the XYZ axis on Google Earth, accounting for spin and any significant intervening geological activity."

I take a deep breath, relieved Billy's on top of this. 'Cause my brain's turned into mush. But the satellite signals—Billy asked something about an echo.

"There was some transmission earlier." Mamma's, I think, wistfully. "We can't rely on it. But we can chart a rough guide by the stars tonight," I say, thinking that if I ever get home I want to go to the Naval Observatory to learn more about how navigators track the night sky. I look up. I have never seen the heavens this bright. Thousands of stars. "Then, we set our time coordinates 520 some-odd years ahead. And *poof!*"

Leo shakes his head in wonder. "How the march of time has expanded man's encyclopedia of knowledge! I would like to observe how these discoveries came to pass."

Seeing my utter exhaustion, Billy must be growing concerned, for he says, "Not now, Leo. Charley and me—we need to have a little talk. Private."

"Of course. And I must see to our machine." Leo bows out in a hurry.

Billy and I are walking arm in arm now. Not twenty-four hours ago, I would have felt stupid about this, but somehow, here, it feels right.

"Seriously, Billy. I'm scared. The awkward conversation I'm going to have to have with Mamma when I get home. Like, 'What's new, Mamma?' and she'd be like, 'Oh, the debut of our composition was a global phenomenon.' And I'd be all, 'Anything you wanna tell me?' And she'd come back with, 'I could ask you the same question!' That's if we even make it back!"

"Don't worry, Charley. We'll figure this out." He pulls a scrap of paper and a nub of pencil from the pants he's wearing under his costume and starts scribbling.

I take a moment to look around, wondering if Lex could be close. That's when I see Carolina determinedly dragging Bethy across the piazza. Bethy, in turn, is dragging Lex's backpack behind her.

"Bethy! You're safe!" The weight that lay like lead across my shoulders is temporarily lifted. "But where is Lex?"

"We were dancing, Carlotta. That is all," Bethy hastens to explain. "When the music stopped, he was swept up in the crowd."

Carolina jumps in, acting out the scene. "Then *Magnifico* returned, storming mad! He called for the strongest men to fight against the silver-tongued prelate. It was Alessandro, er, Lex, who volunteered first!"

Kairos comes over to hear this newest wrinkle. He places a brotherly arm around Carolina.

"I tried to stop him, Carlotta! Lex did not ask for that!" Elisabetta breaks down in sobs.

Well I didn't ask for "the kiss" that sent me here, my first real kiss with a boy. And I didn't ask Lex to follow me here. I didn't ask Bethy II to fall in love with him. I didn't ask Billy to come all the way back in time and rescue me like some damsel in distress.

But here we are, and damn it all—I care about them all, even *my* Bethy, former and maybe someday-again BFF.

"We must get Lex back. There is no time to lose!"

"No need to upset yourself, signorina. I will see to Alessandro's safety," Kairos says, trying to reassure me.

"You don't understand, Kairos! If Lex is taken into *Magnifico*'s army, he may lose his life. And for what? A time, a place, a cause that isn't even his!"

"Oh, but that is where you are wrong, Carlotta. All time is ours."

I grip my head and groan.

"We might even say time does not exist—not as you understand it, in hours and minutes and seconds."

"You don't know what the hell you're talking about, Kairos! We measure it in nanoseconds. It is how we pace progress, place . . . and danger."

"You are slaves to this unreality, then. Time is but a delusion, Carlotta. I *am* Time."

I'm about to go up in flames like Joan of Arc and Kairos is suddenly waxing all philosophical. I mean, what's up with that?

"Here, people live for the moment," he continues, as if not noticing the mirror writing on the wall. "Even the clock on the Duomo is but a reminder to slow down. Notice, its numbers align to sunset! Each week, we adjust it as days lengthen and shorten."

"Fascinating, really, Kairos. But I'm not up for a lecture. *Time. Is. Relative.* Got it."

"Life supplies clock enough. We are born; we die. We live for the seasons and their blessings of sowing, growth, harvesting, and sleep. To take our suppers with our families. To celebrate on feast days. These are the events that give us time. Else we become its prisoners."

Feast day, shmeest day. My stomach starts growling again. A measly handful of grapes is all I've eaten in the past five hundred years, give or take; my stomach is eating away at itself. Wish this place actually were the pasta capital of the world, as advertised.

"Omigod, let's stick with the program here. Otherwise, as of tomorrow I will likely be dunzo-gonzo. Burnt up in the bonfires."

"Carlotta, try to stay, how you say, 'cool'? Remember, each week the clock is reset. They will not even have time to miss you at home."

"Easy for you to say, Kairos!"

Kairos hushes me. "Let us beware. There may be spies among us. Listen!"

It's true, we are hearing a rising buzz. It seems the Weepers are drawing closer. Leonardo, who I can barely make out hurrying back in our direction, must have somehow extracted the tablet from Lex's backpack. He looks up from the screen and motions his head back to point to Lorenzo close behind, an angry look on his face. As he reaches us, Leo passes the tablet to Kairos, who conceals it hastily in the duffel that carries my violin.

The sound of the Weepers grows louder.

"Come with me, all of you." Leonardo mobilizes us. He is apparently in no mood to converse with his patron. "Carlotta, keep away from *Magnifico*. He will no doubt recognize you—and make the association with magic. Quickly! There is no time to lose."

With Lorenzo hurrying toward us on our left flank, his guard from the front, and the Weepers not far behind—there's no way to go but through.

XVIII.
The Ultimate Weapon

Leonardo's plan is for hiding us in plain sight, and it seems to be working. He's like Moses parting the Red Sea: Leo holds up his arms as we trudge through the throngs, keeping our heads down, and the crowd folds in behind us as we depart. This, Savonarola might say, is water. I'm waiting for the Weepers to get drowned in our wake.

But that doesn't happen. We have reached the shadow-cloaked pyramids, those so-called vanities, the ominous mountain of "sin," the tinder for Savonarola's verbal flames.

Billy, still without his glasses, pulls out a flashlight to illuminate our way and immediately regrets it. The beam only acts to show the Weepers where we are.

As the clock on the campanile chimes midnight, we rush to the Ponte Vecchio—me, Billy, Bethy, Kairos, and Leo. My costume, with its flowy skirt, rips, and ruffles, keeps tripping me up. I so want to get back into my real clothes!

Once we get to the rendezvous point near the bridge, I can see that Leonardo has been hard at work reengineering his time machine to do what we need it to do.

But, of course, that could never be completed using only fifteenth-century technology. It's our turn to add some modern bells and whistles and tie them in to other original Leo innovations: gears, chains, and pulleys. Amazing he invented this stuff long before anyone had the tools to actually manufacture them.

Meanwhile, Billy and I are busy retrofitting our solar antenna with the servomotor. We've adapted a Lego bot, which Billy had the foresight to stuff into his duffel, and attached a rudely fashioned solar-, fire-, and wind-propelled engine. This Rube Goldberg–like contraption features a lever that can be tripped by Leonardo's dropping a hail of rocks into his new-and-improved catapult.

"Where are the tri-barrels, Leonardo?" I ask, feeling ever greater urgency as the Weepers continue their wailing in the distance. "We'll need as much firepower as possible. Where will they be positioned?"

"In the piazza, where they have set up the scaffold for the Florentines' amusements," he says with a grimace. And by amusements, I'm getting that I'd be headlining (no pun intended!).

"Yes, I believe this could do it. Fingers crossed!"

I see Bethy crossing her fingers and everything else.

"Billy, what about the Qualia Rosetta? 'Cause, frankly, if the formula's off, we might just as well end up in Ancient Egypt with Cleopatra. Or on Mars with the Curiosity rover."

"Working out the math, Charley. Give me a sec," he says.

"I think our time machine needs a name, Billy. Let's call it Curiosity 2.0."

"Got it all loaded on the tablet, Charley. We will just have to trust that, as Kairos says, the second golden compass, inserted in the lock on Horse and Rider, will activate the Qualia Rosetta. From that point, all we can do is wait for the sun to be at its peak tomorrow. Pray it doesn't rain. I've calculated that with the boosted solar power, plus Leonardo's cannon fire, and, hopefully, a few rogue fireworks—"

"*Si!*" Bethy II affirms. "It is also the day of the bonfire of the vanities."

I get an idea. It will be tricky, but it's our best hope. "Bethy, we'll need your help. You and I must be captured—to get them parading through the main piazza—music, flares, floats, and all."

"But this is so dangerous!" Bethy exclaims.

"Whatever! We'll need to distract the crowd while Leonardo, Billy, and Kairos set up the machine. The crowd wants witchcraft? We will give them witchcraft!"

I see the fear welling up in her eyes.

"Think of it as saving Lexy."

"For Lexy," she repeats robotically.

Leonardo breaks in. "*Silencio!* We must cloak this catapult somehow to hide it in plain sight and move it into position in the piazza before the sun's peak tomorrow."

"Like the stealth bomber," I say.

"Stealth? This is an advanced cannon in your time?" asks Leonardo.

"Jet fighter plane. Like your drawing of the flying machine?" Billy looks practically jubilant. "This is undoubtedly gonna be the greatest virtual reality game I will ever someday invent! Leo, you're a genius, man!"

As for me, I'll hold off on popping the champagne until I see that this "experiment" actually works. So many lives now depend on it, that I have to believe.

"Right. While you guys are lugging the gear to set up in the piazza, Bethy and I can find enough cloth and stuff to disguise everything until we need to unveil our ultimate weapon."

I palm the golden compass and spit on it for good luck. Bethy leans over to spit too. Billy rubs it clean with a shirtsleeve before handing it back to me. "Germs!"

I laugh out loud for the first time in eons: Some things never change.

"C'mon, Bethy," I say as I stash the compass in my backpack for safe-keeping. "Our work here is vital. For truth!"

"For Lexy. *Mi amore!*" she seconds. With that, we scurry off to scavenge.

XIX.
What Hath Time Wrought?

Because Bethy knows the lay of the land, I follow her lead. We need lengths of cloth, tarps, hay, dried wildflowers, weeds—anything that will drape our ultimate weapon in its own costume. A second Mardi Gras masquerade.

It feels like a fool's mission. Then again, what are we humans if not all fools and dreamers who create our own futures, choice by choice?

We enter a storehouse not far from the *campo* where I first touched down. Outside, sheep and goats are sleeping. Inside are bales and bales of wool. The hay smells so good and the wool so inviting, that I sit down, unable to move any farther. My foot is aching again.

It's been a long day. "You go, Bethy. I need to rest my feet."

She raises an eyebrow. "You will be safe here, Carlotta?"

I look around. It's quiet. The light of the moon streams in through slits in the wooden walls. There is no Savonarola, no *Magnifico*, no one expecting me to solve the problems of the world. "Safe. Yes, so safe."

She hesitates before continuing the search for cloaking materials.

I rifle through my backpack and see the glint of the golden compass. The key to saving me. And now, Billy and Lex too. Fingers crossed. I curl my fingers around it and then drop it in my pocket. A talisman.

Digging out my phone, I pray it holds enough juice to tap out a new blog post. Maybe my last.

Blog Entry #7. For My Eyes Only.

On the night before I am fated to stand trial for witch-craft, I look up again at the heavens. There's a brilliant sliver of moon. It wasn't there last night but has come out to witness my death—for what offense, I do not know! Is this the same moon that shines outside my window in Takoma Park? Is Dad staring up at the sky, wondering what will become of his little girl? And Mamma: Does this shiny crescent hang over her as she steps outside after the concert? Does she worry about her cara Carlotta as I worry about her? I'm sorry, Mamma!

I judge from the phone's hourglass that the sands are quickly running out. I am so scared, my heart is racing. Oh, if only I could be home now, snug in my bed, knowing that the ones I love are nearby! To have even one more sleepover with Beth—MY Beth, once and future BFF. We'd paint our toes and giggle and gossip about Lex all night long. I'd forgive her all her annoyingness a million times over to not carry our fighting in my heart!

What seemed so real now feels like a dream. Meeting the maestro himself, getting to know the man behind the myth?

Priceless.

How could I imagine my little ambition would set my entire life into a tailspin? I could know everything but what is in the hearts of the people around me. Not knowing my own. Besides Dad and Mamma, only Billy seems to have no ulterior motive. And I used to take him for granted!

Where once, winning the science fair seemed the only important thing in the world, I've learned it means little in the long horizon of time. Misplaced priorities, Dad would call them. It took me 500 years and twenty-four hours to learn that lesson.

It's probably a moot point. Tomorrow, my hands will be tied. "Strega," they call me. Bethy II says that they will place a burlap sack over my head and tie me to the stake. Acrid smoke may choke me as the fire is set. The dance of flames will lick at my feet and the dance of fear at my heart. What a horrible way to die. Worse, Bethy is also innocent, yet she may be punished for my knowledge.

Perhaps the stars will continue to shine five hundred years from now through the light pollution of Washington's suburbs and over my neighborhood, my street, my house. These points of light are meant to outshine us all. We are not the center of anything. Light will continue to lift the darkness of ignorance that shrouds humanity in smog. It will survive us all.

What will happen once I die? Will anyone know this story? Maybe it doesn't matter. If I had never lived, I would not have caused Mamma all that worry, would not have disturbed history with my ideas out of time. But I also would have missed out on the experience of a lifetime.

My blog is my codex. If you see this, dear reader—if you are struck in any way by my tale of passion and pretense, progress and portent, pride and prudence, I invite you to reach for your own star, no matter the cost.

The journey is its own reward.

And if Fortune does indeed smile upon me, it is my dearest
wish to be able to tell Mamma and Dad in person how much I
love them. And my baby brother(s)- or sister(s)-to-be.

If the future is still mine—someday, somehow—I swear!
You will see me there.

Bethy's shaking me. "Carlotta! It is done. The sun is well above the horizon. It is time!"

"Whoa. Must've fallen asleep. How long was I out?" I ask, rubbing my eyes.

"Hurry!" She pulls me from my cozy woolen bed, grabs my backpack, and we start out at a run. The sun shines high above us as we scurry back into Firenze. Beggars tail us; men are sleeping off their drunkenness from last night, slumped against the homes, shops, and guilds lining the way.

Elisabetta throws a cloak over me so my face is shadowed beneath the hood. She is similarly cloaked now—for she, too, is under suspicion.

Outside the Pitti Palace, Lorenzo sits mounted on horseback, hounded by citizens petitioning him to rid Florence of sinners. He is conferring with a man who looks just like him.

A familiar orator harangues the crowd from on high. Savonarola is once more perched above the bonfire of the vanities on the piazza, conspiring openly with his Weepers about the wickedness infesting the city. "Sorcerers and witches cast a spell upon our rulers!" and the crowd replies, "Let them prove their innocence!"

Leonardo joins *Magnifico* in the huddle. Are they conspiring? Would that be for or against me? Surely the ruler of Florence has ultimate say in a witch hunt!

Bethy and I approach the venerated rulers of Florence. I am huffing and puffing out of exertion and fear. "Where is Billy?" I ask.

The third man, who I now notice wears the collar and garb of the priesthood, barely acknowledges us. "Father, they call for blood. The Church will not tolerate heretics."

Wracking my brain for context, I surmise this must be Lorenzo's son Giovanni de' Medici, a cardinal, and future Pope Leo X.

Lorenzo replies, "Giovanni, these children are strangers to our customs. And since da Vinci has taken them under his wing . . ." He looks to Leonardo, who nods.

"But they stir the passions of the people. An example must be made!" Giovanni, for a future pope, doesn't appear to have much sympathy.

Leonardo walks behind Bethy and me. He puts his arms around us like a blessing and slips my backpack off my shoulder. "I will take this for safekeeping," he says with a wink. Leaning in closer, he whispers, "The plan is set." He points surreptitiously to a large pile disguised by the wool, hay, and straw that Bethy must have gathered while I was sleeping. It is positioned in between the two pyramids heaped with Florence's "vanities," their treasures.

"Fear not," he assures us with a grim smile. "You will be reunited anon with all those who await you!"

"From your mouth to God's ears!" I whisper as Leonardo strides away. And although I am not a Believer, so far in my life these words are the closest I have come to a prayer.

The crowd is swelling. Firecrackers set off by the Weepers alight dangerously close to our small huddle. Out of safety concerns for the Republic, or fearing, perhaps, for his own safety, Lorenzo gives the command to his guards: "Seize these girls, these heretics who inflame the hearts of my citizens!"

None other than Viola grabs us as Bethy shrieks, "NO! *Prego*, my cousin!"

Despite this being part of the plan, I flinch at being so accused. I wish they could hear the truth! Without a word, Viola ties our hands and ushers us to the center of the piazza. We march through a sea of people. The day's festivities represent a veritable circus: parades, floats, jesters, and jugglers. Wandering bards regale listeners with stories, and minstrels offer musical interludes. I even spot children gathered around a miniature stage, laughing at the marionettes in a Punch and Judy show, *Pulcinella*.

Show horses draped in official-looking coats of arms and led by their equally colorfully garbed riders probably signal races later in the day. In the distance, I see a full paddock of the magnificent horses awaiting Lorenzo's signal. Would that I could jump on one and run free!

But such is not meant to be. Viola is leading us to a cart. "You will be driven around the piazza," she informs us robotically. "*Il Magnifico* decrees it so."

"Yeah, well, nice knowing you, too, Viola," I mutter, pulling my hood further over my face. Sentinels surround us, spears and swords drawn. Like some outdoor medieval torture chamber, we are facing a wall of weapons.

I wonder if Viola will at least show Bethy some mercy, but, no; it looks like my Florentine BFF will not be spared. Maybe Viola has no choice: Who knows what threats she is under?

Two other hooded girls climb aboard our circus wagon. So we aren't the only witches threatening the future of Firenze! As we are paraded around the square, I hang my head in shame. I remind myself I have done nothing wrong!

I peek out from under my hood as the crowd cheers: Giovanni de' Medici is regally entering the piazza, bowing and waving his golden cardinal's staff. I have to squint as it glints off the torches and catches the rays of the bright noontime sun.

My nerves are getting the better of me. I chew on my pinkie nail. Mamma would remind me about my bad habits. I think about Mamma being in the Florence of her time. I know she's looking for me. She's probably playing our music, hoping to open that window again that allowed us a glimpse of each other.

What would Mamma say if she could see this spectacle? For once, I am glad my tablet is dead.

In the distance, I spy Leonardo and Kairos walking swiftly through the throngs gathering around us. Perhaps it is only my imagination, but it is almost as if I can hear Kairos lamenting that things have come to this.

"Poor Carlotta. Her only sin is curiosity, and a compulsion to speak her mind. She would fare better to keep silent. Speech is a crime for a maid such as her."

"But it is not so in her own time, it would appear," Leonardo argues. "It has long since come to my attention that people of accomplishment rarely sit back and let things happen to them. They go out and happen to things."

"Still, we must do something, maestro. These maidens are accused of witchery. They will be flogged and locked in the pillory—or worse!"

Yes, do something! Whose brilliant idea was it to be publicly accused, anyway?

A crowd walks alongside our cart. Looking forward, I see we're approaching the platform in the center of the piazza. Awaiting us is a group of Savonarola's Weepers. Savonarola is preaching to the crowd about virtue and godliness. Spectators begin throwing pebbles at the wagon as we pass.

A young boy is hopping alongside our cart, priming his slingshot. He seems to find a continuous reserve of rocks and pebbles along the path to shoot at us. One such missile looks to be headed right in between me and Elisabetta, but she's looking the other way. I push her down and throw myself over her for protection.

"THAT'S IT!" I yell at the pest. "YOU'RE NOT GOING TO GET US, YOU BULLY!" I throw off my hood, suddenly without fear. After all, what are they going to do: kill me? I stare defiantly over the crowd even as it swells with growing intensity, answering the passions of Savonarola.

". . . You need also to remove these poems, games, and taverns, and the evil customs in women's dress." Savonarola stops and glares in our direction.

The cart comes to a halt mere yards from the fiery preacher. As we are pushed from the cart, Elisabetta is counting her rosary, sobbing, prayers constant on her lips. At sword point, we are forced to mount the steps, rising laboriously above the crowd. Slowly, we come face-to-face with our demise.

"Everything harmful to the soul's health must be banished," spews Savonarola from the platform above us. He holds out his hands toward his pyramids: exhibits A and B. The anger and fear blistering off the masses beneath us is overwhelming.

As he surveys his vanities, his eye rests momentarily on exhibit C— our stealth weapon. If he is surprised at its presence, it doesn't show.

Ignoring the fact for the moment that this is our plan set into motion, I dig in my heels. "I demand to see a lawyer! This is a civilized country—whatever happened to innocent until proven guilty?!"

I pull out the hand mirror I have secreted in my dress pocket and shine it in the eyes of Lorenzo's men. The guards answer by grabbing me tightly under the arms and dragging me forward. They attempt to grab the mirror away, but their gloved hands make it difficult to grasp. I manage to pocket it before they can hit the mirror to the ground.

I smell the smoke, feel the heat of the bonfires, as all four of us are being pushed, pulled, and prodded toward our fate, our bodies trembling.

Our arms are draped over a long horizontal post and our wrists are bound. I am just able to again take out my mirror, which I grasp tightly, even as my hands start tingling from loss of circulation. As one of the unknown accused girls crumbles, I try to stand taller in defiance.

My heart is racing so fast, I'm sure it's gonna jump right out from under my rib cage. *C'mon, Charley. Have faith! It's all gonna work.*

Billy and Leo are nowhere to be seen. Even Kairos the Omnipresent is absent.

What comes next looks to have been a long time in the planning, long before our captivity. A sea of young boys all in white surrounds our platform. More lighted torches surround the mountains of luxuries, flames glinting and dancing off the gold and mirrors. A chorus of singers and musicians performs Lorenzo's musical compositions for Carnevale.

Music for the soul, I imagine, with a bitter laugh at the irony of it all. "How could this have happened?" I say to no one in particular. "I wanted to be part of the famous flowering of the Firenze Renaissance. Instead, her citizens are throwing things at us. Calling us names!"

"With or without an edict from *Magnifico*, the crowd could kill us," Bethy whispers. "Pray that *Dio* will spare us!"

The crowd is chanting, "*Strega!* Devil worshippers! Heretics!" As the shouting fuels discord among them, the volume escalates until the music is drowned out.

Trial by fire. Literally! Who would've thought such a punishment might befall me. After all, what did I do wrong? "Since when is curiosity a crime!" I demand, even as we are being pelted by stones. "This is so unreal!"

"What are you talking about? These stones are real!" Elisabetta cries. "The fire that will burn us is real! Perhaps it is true what they say and you really are a witch who will not feel any pain."

"I am not a witch," I say. "Nor are you! But quantum physics predicts that what we see as reality is more like a hologram. Like a virtual reality game."

I wish Billy, inventive game maker that he is, were here to confirm my hypothesis. It's a hope I must cling to. It's all I have left.

Savonarola watches dispassionately as the guards march us to the higher platform where we come face-to-face with our accuser. I am determined to look him unflinchingly in the eye, if only I can hold my head up. We are positioned in front of four pillories that are attached to a tall post, like spokes coming off a wheel. Before they make us put our arms and heads into the holes, I quick grab the compass out of my pocket and tuck it securely in my sleeve when the guards aren't looking. My arms are suspended over my shoulders, and I can scarcely move my head. Not exactly a comfortable position.

Now we are four girls stationed in four directions: spring, summer, fall, and winter, each playing a seasonal role in purification. Elisabetta is whimpering. The other two girls are stoic. I try not to think about what will happen next. It's a game I must play—counting my blessings, listing all the things I am grateful for: Mamma, Dad, Billy, Lex. Beth. Leonardo, Kairos, Elisabetta, Carolina. Life itself. But other thoughts keep filtering in: What's going to happen to us? Why are these other girls accused? Where's Billy now? Is our plan going to work? Are we going to die?

"No, Charley," I tell myself. "Focus on what you're going to do next: How the hell am I going to grab the compass from up my sleeve? How can I adjust the angle of the mirror?" I fight to keep my monkey mind in check.

Below me, I spy priceless treasures stacked into the pile to be burned: Botticelli, Michelangelo, Dante, da Vinci. They have been designated as kindling for a nefarious purpose: to set us on fire!

I twist my head and raise my eyes as far as I can while my head is locked into a hole. I notice how they've discretely uncloaked da Vinci's beautiful machine. It stands higher than our platform . . . as high as the vanities! To me, at this moment, the time machine my friends assembled during the night is more beautiful than all the gold, trinkets, and masterpieces in Florence!

Beside our machine, I see a glinting from mirrors reflecting at multiple angles and aimed in a focal point toward our makeshift solar panel to magnify the sun's rays and create enough energy to—hope against hope!—activate our machine.

I catch a glint to my right: Billy is right below me. He is aiming the second compass from the direction opposite the machine to magnify the force. I wiggle my hand, trying to shake my compass out of my sleeve and into my sweaty palm.

"Behold! The sword of the Lord will descend suddenly and quickly upon the earth," thunders Savonarola. At that, Lorenzo's guards form two facing rows and cross swords in salute.

The air is stifling, with rising smoke. Have they lit the bonfire?

If I can lift my hands, and angle the mirror and compass just so, maybe, maybe I can create a laser beam strong enough to trigger the solar panel atop the time machine. The plan is for Billy et al. to charge in and release us with enough time to run for the tepee/time machine. The Operation Firenze tablet is affixed, and should count down to a preset launch code. I pray it is programmed using the correct coordinates to reverse the Qualia Rosetta so that, if the gods are in our favor, we will have created enough force to catch a ride home.

I manage to find the light with my mirror—first the sun, then the flames—but I can't draw them into a point of light together, and not with enough force. My hands are shaking. "Steady, Charley!" I coach myself. "Deep breaths now."

I'm praying for the second time in my life: "Please work!" Leo said we needed to gather all the forces together—a singular point of light to direct with laser-like intensity to trigger the time machine. I try again. And again. Until finally, "There! This may catch it!" I squeeze my eyes tight. "Please work. Please work. Please work!"

What if combining the flames and aiming the beam at the panel is not enough to activate the machine? Or worse yet, what if our aim is off, and instead of the time machine, it sparks the tinderbox platform where we've been bound?

I am in the hands of Fate.

I hear the hooves of horses and voices screaming like banshees. My eyes pop open and I crane my neck to see.

"CHARLEY!!!! WE'RE COMING TO GET YOU!" Billy, Lex, and Kairos are leading the charge on the ruler's magnificent white stallions. Billy's wearing his Nats cap again, but otherwise, the three are dressed as jesters, the better to blend in as part of the day's festivities. Wasn't Billy just below me?

Behind them, Leonardo's tank, to which his multi-barreled cannons

are now attached, lumbers its way slowly through the piazza. Modeled after a turtle but with a removable shell, no one has ever seen the likes of this before; seeing it advancing toward them, the formerly angry crowd disperses in terror. Leonardo himself leads the way.

"Hold on, Charley! We're coming!" Lex whoops and hollers. And Kairos the Omnipresent, looking all *calmo*, grins.

"LEXY!" Bethy screams. "Lexy, save me!"

I roll my eyes at the helpless princess act and her new Knight in Baggy Sweatpants coming to save her. But it doesn't matter: I see color in her cheeks again. I wish I could reach over to try to squeeze her hand.

In a strong tenor, Billy begins to sing. "O beautiful, for spacious skies / For amber waves of grain . . ."

"America the Beautiful." At this moment, I couldn't agree more.

Leonardo scrambles down from his watchtower atop the tank, wildly swinging a halberd and roaring like a lion to clear out the now-distracted guards. He runs right up to Savonarola, and the preacher relinquishes his open-air pulpit without a fight.

What an out-of-body experience! Here I am, about to be burned at the stake, watching myself and all the chaos unfolding. Then again, I try to comfort myself, it's hardly weirder than everything else that's happened on this journey.

A handful of ragtag boys is assembling beneath us—kids who don't seem to be a part of the official festivities. Have I seen them before?

"Look, Carlotta," Bethy nods her head. "Those boys! They were cockfighting yesterday by the Arno!"

So it would seem. Somehow I remember Bethy flirting and playing with them too. And Wilbur. Poor little pig. But that was before Sexy Lexy arrived.

This crazy little band doesn't appear to have a leader, until one small, boyish figure detaches from the pack and calls out to us.

"'Betta! *Tcharr-li!* I am here!" It is none other than Carolina in boy's clothing, to our defense.

Carolina leads the boys to the paddock, where the horses buck and snort restlessly. They let loose *il Magnifico*'s horses and mount the stolen steeds. Boldly, the young horse thieves charge through the crowds, riding figure eights around the vast pyramids, our stealth weapon, and the platform.

Amid the chaos, Billy and Lex climb the wooden steps to where we are held hostage. They brandish nothing more ferocious than pocketknives. Deftly, Billy figures out how to release the pillory. He isn't on track for Eagle Scout for nothing! Lex simultaneously frees Elisabetta, his damsel in distress.

Just in time. A hooded monk standing below us holds the torch meant to ignite the bonfire of the vanities. At that moment, the fireworks that had been set for the close of the Mardi Gras festivities explode unpredictably all around. If fireworks are dangerous in our time, imagine Roman candles, comets, and Chinese lanterns dotting the piazza where everything is tinder. Some fizzle. More explode.

The piazza empties out amid screams and random blasts and misfires. We, too, take heel. Billy and Kairos grab the reins of two of the ruling family's horses and ride quickly over to assemble with us at the edge of the piazza.

Kairos hands Billy his duffel bag. I pray my violin is still safely tucked inside.

"Hey, thanks, man," Billy says. "You're a lifesaver."

"I am but an apprentice of the great master," Kairos says with undue humility.

Leonardo emerges from his makeshift turtle-tank and hurries over, carrying my backpack.

"Here is your sack, Carlotta. I believe we have cracked the time

code, thanks to you. Hurry! The window is closing to get back to your own time."

"Thank you, maestro. You have taught me so much. I am forever grateful."

I am surprised when the Greatest Genius the World Has Ever Known takes my hand and kisses it. "And you, Carlotta? What have you taken from this experiment?"

"That you, Ser Leonardo, through all your scientific observation and amazing inventions, have left a legacy to the future that we're just beginning to understand. That even when everything we need to know is right in front of our eyes, wisdom cannot be unlocked before we are ready to receive it."

Leonardo nods in appreciation. "You are wise, Carlotta. This is a lesson few people have truly absorbed, in my time or any other. Make haste, before time runs out!"

"*Mille grazie, Ser Leonardo,*" I say, suddenly sorry our time together will be ending.

With a bow, Leonardo runs back toward his tank, undoubtedly to prime the cannons.

Savonarola's voice rings out over the crowd. "If God wills it, those accused must show how they walk through fire!" He still mesmerizes with his words.

I pull Billy by the hand. "Time to bolt, guys." But Lex isn't moving. "We're out of here. Lex? Coming?"

He balks. "Um, well . . . no. I believe I'll stick around this place awhile. It's better than a video game . . . or some lame science experiment at school. And then, there's Elisabetta . . ."

A wilted Bethy II smiles weakly and leans her head against Lex. He turns, brushes her hair off his face and grins.

"Don't be an idiot, Lex," says Billy. "You're in danger here. Plus, there's the paradox problem: If you stay here, you've opened the door to an alternate future. We have to get back—all of us."

Elisabetta takes Lex's hand and pats it. "I will protect him! We will run away together. To Rome! Right, Lexy? No one there will know us." She throws her arms around him. If Lex was undecided before, there's no changing his course now.

"You're *pazzi*. Both of you," I scold. Crazy Lexy.

"Wait, I need to give you something." I nervously begin to sort through my backpack, where I find the maquette, wrapped in Leonardo's folio paper, with sketches and mirror writing covering the page. What souvenirs! But then, at the bottom, I find what I am looking for: my lucky Susan B. Anthony dollar.

"Here you go, guys. For luck."

Then I lock my golden compass into the maquette, praying Billy still has the other, and salute its live model one final time. "Thank you,

Kairos! Someday, I'll understand your magic."

"I have no doubt you will someday, kid!" he winks.

"To the time machine!" Billy exclaims. "Say, Charley, you want a bite of my sandwich? For energy?"

"Wow, yes! Even cardboard might taste good right now."

He grins as he pulls the PB&J out of his duffel. Thank goodness it's not baloney. (Alas, poor Wilbur!) I'm thinking of becoming a vegetarian. Leonardo is, you know!

This peanut butter picnic in the shadow of the Ponte Vecchio as fireworks flare all around us might even be romantic, if our situation weren't so dire.

As the rockets blast around us, I half expect to hear the musicians take up the climax of Tchaikovsky's 1812 Overture, which would nicely punctuate the pending cannon fire. Except, of course, it hasn't been written yet. Instead, Lorenzo's musicians clamorously pick out a somewhat shaky yet triumphal reprise of "Leo."

Somewhere in the cosmos, in sync with the live music, plays a sort of simultaneous echo, slightly out of pitch yet familiar and oddly ethereal: my duet with Mamma—playing across time!

If music be a portal to the cosmos, play it 'til the heavens sing.

Billy and I lace our fingers together and dash across the piazza, under rockets' red glare. When the third cannon around the tank echoes its thundering nine-gun salute, Billy kisses me, and I brace myself for the physical pull that happened with Lex. But this is not the same feeling.

As I realize that this new sensation isn't so much on the outside as on my insides, suddenly the cannons' firing in spiral sequence reverses. Once again, I feel the Tilt-a-Whirl that—fingers crossed!—will blast us home.

As the whirling vortex sweeps us up, I shout, *"Arrivederci,* Firenze!"

But I have a funny feeling I will be here again. In time.

Before the wind, light, and explosions entirely engulf us, I see Leonardo taking long, hurried strides into the same field of energy that encompasses us. And who is the small boy skipping beside him—but no!

Leonardo and Carolina are about to walk right out of time.

XX.
WHERE AM I?

Straightaway, we are in motion; forces of gravity squeeze my heart and lungs inside my chest in cosmic winds. An ethereal, white light wraps around us. The cosmic forces are beginning to feel familiar. I pry open one eyelid against the centrifugal force to make sure Billy's still here; the universe is playing my song.

And then—BOOM!

Another hard landing.

I snuggle my head against my arms and tense my body, prepared—or as prepared as anyone ever can be—for a rocket blast, the explosion of cannons, flames licking my feet.

Dead. Silence.

I lift my head and open one eye. It's dark. Where am I? Did it work?

At first, all I hear is my own heart beating and my breath in my ears, but rising underneath it is a dull "Mwah, mwah-mwah, mwah-mwah."

What's up with the cartoon voices? I'm sooo dizzy. I shake my head to clear out the fog, and the shapes around me seem to melt into familiarity. My eyes adjust as the darkness lightens, and at last my gaze focuses on the periodic table of elements.

It's still on the dark side, but Curiosity 2.0 has landed: I am definitely in sixth period at Da Vinci Middle School and—thank god!—Billy is at our lab table beside me. We're sitting in science class, and no wonder it's still dark: The shades are drawn and lights are out so that everyone can see the PowerPoint projections and video presentations on the SMART Board.

That means it's the day to pitch our ideas for the science fair.

Which means it's two days before the day that changed my life forever. *Miracolo.*

Beth is just finishing her presentation and sits two tables away in her assigned seat. Alone. Seems her project is no longer about marigolds and music—something about practicing yoga as a way to calm the chattering teen brain for developing greater focus.

Wait! Is this the same drama queen Beth who so recently ran away from a sleepover in the middle of the night *over a boy?*

And where's Lex?

Then I remember: Lex stayed behind. A paradox. In all likelihood, he may never have existed here.

Billy's got on earbuds beneath his Nats cap. My tablet is open in front of him, and his duffel is under our table.

"Was that a dream?" I whisper.

"That was the realest reality ever," he whispers and turns the tablet to face me.

At the front of the room, Mrs. Schreiber is working to keep the presentations on time. "Let's see, who'll go next?" she thrums her fingers on her desk.

Hands go up. I slouch low, trying to look inconspicuous. I'm still trying to work out what just happened. Doing a mental accounting, I realize that it's not just Lex who's out of time now. Leonardo looked like he had his own plan set on our departure. And where in the world could Carolina think she'd be going?!

Beth points at me with a beatific smile and a gleam in her eyes. "I think we should hear from Charley, Mrs. Schreiber. She and Billy have come up with *the most interesting* experiment!"

"Charlotte?" It's Mrs. Schreiber, calling me to attention. "You're up next. You and William."

I glance at Beth to see if she's being sincere or snarky. Not sure what to make of her at this moment.

"Sure, Mrs. Schreiber. Billy Vincenzo and I have decided to delve into the science of longevity."

I steal a glance back at Billy, whose face registers surprise before he ducks back to the tablet, where I trust he will dig up something to bail us out.

"Um . . . yeah. Well . . ."

C'mon, Charley, I tell myself. You came out of one dangerous scrape alive. You can do this!

"Women have made some significant advances in science," I start, composing myself. "And Dr. Elizabeth Blackburn is one of only a handful of women who have won the Nobel Prize in Medicine. She's a pioneer in cell biology for her work on telomerase. Which is about extending the life of cells. And aging in humans," I add, thankful that, a lifetime ago, I had read that article and expounded on Dr. Blackburn's research to Bethy.

I'm deliberately trying to talk slowly, but then Billy pokes me, grinning. "Yeah. Tell 'em our hypothesis, Charley."

If I could only think of what that might be. "Um, so the question might be whether we can discover a way to reverse aging of the body, which, when combined with AI and big data, could lead to cognitive computing—a cyber clone of us—giving each of us a sort of digital immortality." Living forever is just another form of time travel, after all.

I hear murmurs and chuckles from the class. "Sure, Charley—Fountain of Youth."

Doubters!

"No, really, check this out, guys!" Beth chimes in breathlessly. Out of the corner of my eye, I see her rifling through the latest fashion issue of *Vogue*, which is like Beth's bible. "It says right here: Stress is apparently a big factor in aging. And my project, on yoga, is about reducing stress!"

My mouth drops. This, coming from *fashionista* Beth! What if . . . when Lex is out of the picture . . . ? Now that might be a real paradox.

But I can't think about that.

"Nice observation, Elizabeth. Perhaps you, Charlotte, and William could collaborate on your efforts," suggests Mrs. Schreiber.

Impulsively, Beth jumps up to give me a hug, which I hesitantly return. With Billy, it's more triumphal: We trade fist bumps.

And when I open my fist, a Golden Compass is inside.

POSTSCRIPT

I f anyone but Billy had shown me what was unfolding on the live video stream on my tablet, I would've doubted that anything I'd experienced in the past twenty-four or so hours was real. In fact, I still had to ask him after class if he'd recorded it, so I could watch it, sound up, uninterrupted. After all, from the glimpse I saw, it could've been an episode of *Doctor Who*, or part of the History channel series *Ancient Aliens*. Or some other pseudoscientific reenactment.

As soon as school is over, I grab my bike and pedal as hard as I can for home. The minute I walk in the door, I am greeted by the screech of some little kid's violin lesson.

"Mamma? I'm home!" I yell as soon as there's a nanosecond's break in the noise, and hold my breath.

"Help yourself to the spaghetti pomodoro in the fridge, Charley," she calls back.

Nothing short of normal in that. Was this all a figment of my imagination?

"Oh, and Charley, I have something to share with you later. Amazing news!" she adds as an afterthought.

Which amazing news could that be? I ask myself nervously, running through the possibilities in my brain—NSO tour in Italy; Take Your Child to Work Day time hack; new baby brothers and/or sisters. How to respond? Would I be all, like, "Hunh. Tell me something I don't know!" or "Great news!" or "That sucks."

But even as I review the options, my hunger overwhelms me. Unable to wait a second longer, I scarf down the spaghetti, cold, straight from the container. Ironic that in Takoma Park, Maryland, U.S.A., you can find better pasta than in old *Italia* itself!

As soon as I've licked the plastic clean, I run and lock myself in my room, crawling into my hiding space in the eaves, the better to binge watch without distractions.

And so, friends, Florentines, and da Vinci fans everywhere, here is the whole, unadulterated, interactive transcript and description of what Billy captured streaming live—a singular moment in time.

Fake news or not, I leave it to you.

Leonardo da Vinci emerges in someone's old-fashioned (for my time) kitchen. On the table, there's a local newspaper opened to an ad—it's in

German, I think, with all those long compound words. But I can read the date: Bern, Switzerland, 1905, and the name, Albert Einstein.

Einstein!

I'd heard Einstein kept a messy office, but this is ridiculous: papers and books strewn across every square inch of space.

We see the back of the famous scientist's trademark mane as the two geniuses come face-to-face. Between da Vinci and Einstein, that's gotta be some bad hair day.

Einstein does not seem surprised to see da Vinci; in fact, one might think these two are old friends.

That chameleon-like IT guy extraordinaire Kairos appears: Apparently, in this epoch, he is Einstein's assistant. Kairos holds the Horse and Rider maquette that Billy and I just used to get home.

What?! I hit pause and quick dig through my backpack—laden with the dirt, detritus, and rocks an archeologist might find layers deep in the Tuscan sediment. Finding my dead phone, I plug it in to charge, and the hourglass has been replaced—not with digits, or even ye olde analog clock, but by the famously restored original clock face from the campanile in Florence herself.

And then I get to the sheaf of papers Leonardo used to wrap the maquette. I unfold these gingerly—careful not to tear, smudge, or otherwise mutilate these priceless souvenirs from Leonardo's original codices—but I already know what I'm going to find. The miniature sculpture of Horse and Rider is missing. The wonders of Kairos never cease.

I continue playing the video, anxious to hear what two of the world's most brilliant people have on their minds. A capstone to our very own *casus mirabilis*, Billy and I are flies on the wall, witnessing an unheard of encounter between the Renaissance man and the person who ushered in the Atomic Age, with Kairos serving as interpreter:

ALBERT EINSTEIN: The only reason for time is so that everything doesn't happen at once.
LEONARDO DA VINCI: I am told that you are responsible for determining the speed of light and the curvature of space?
EINSTEIN: I have merely posited that space-time is a continuum. And that objects having mass—even particles at the quantum level—cannot surpass light speed.
LEONARDO: Ah, that, *miei amici*, is but the tip of the iceberg. I have two young friends who assure me that one day, some hundred years hence, an elusive particle predicted later in your twentieth century will do us one better. Look here, Alberto . . .

Einstein and Leonardo put their heads together, marveling over the world they see emerge on . . . a tablet?!

I hit pause on the recording to allow this news to register:

Dad's tablet! In Leonardo da Vinci's and Albert Einstein's hands. And relativity still only a draft theoretical paper in Einstein's patent office.

I whistle my uneasiness. How am I ever gonna explain *this* to Dad!

EINSTEIN: You mean they will in fact confirm the standard model, my friend?

LEONARDO: I hear that they will have constructed miles of tunnels beneath the ground we are standing on to create a facsimile of its properties. They call it the "God particle." Though, in my day, the Church would deem all that I have seen in recent days heresy, and this new evidence a blasphemy. Still, I have learned that without this Godly manifestation, dubbed the Higgs boson, objects could have no mass. They say the "Higgs field" is like the water the entire universe swims in. We bathe in an ocean of energy.

EINSTEIN: The most beautiful thing we can experience is the mysterious. It is the source of all true art and all science. So, our task must be to widen our circle of compassion to embrace all living creatures and the whole of nature in its beauty.

LEONARDO: And seeing ourselves across time can help us gain the perspective that we are but seeds of that creation. Our visit here today is proof.

EINSTEIN: Indeed. It's about time, da Vinci. About time.

I video chat my co-conspirator. "We've got a problem, Billy. My dad's tablet is gone—back in time with Leo and Einstein!"

"Tell you the truth, Charley? Nothing surprises me anymore."

"What are we going to do about it?"

"Do?" He raises one eyebrow. "What is there to do?"

I am not even referring to the unhistorical fact of the two greatest geniuses of all time gabbing over coffee. Or that Leonardo apparently engineered the settings for his own time travel using our technology to hitchhike on our ride home by way of 1905 Switzerland, Einstein's so-called annus mirabilis, the year of wonders!

"Think, Billy—the future of the world is at stake! Not to mention my own. What am I gonna do about Dad's tablet and Operation Firenze? The FBI could put Dad in jail if they find out!" I fidget with my copy of the golden compass.

"Back to the edge of yesterday?" he suggests with a grin.

I grin back. "For our next adventure, Webhead? Are you ready?"

"Well, I do like antique technologies. Besides, what's the worst that could happen?" He raises a hand to show me his copy of the golden compass.

"Yippee! Fingers crossed, Billy!" I hold mine up to show him. "This is gonna be epic!"

ROBIN STEVENS PAYES is a social marketing consultant and science writer specializing in reaching—and decoding—teen brains. She dove headfirst into parenting teens when her three kids were trying their wings and testing their limits.

Since her passion is storytelling, she relished listening in on backseat conversations between her children and their friends. As her kids grew, Payes tuned in to how their language, ideas, and attitudes transformed along with their bodies and brains. The exercise represented a complete anthropological study in teen social psychology. For a mom, teens may be lovable and exasperating, but for a writer and science interpreter? Priceless.

Payes lives in Rockville, Maryland, where she works with teens on STEAM learning—science, technology, engineering, arts and design, and math—and consults with readers on creating new apps, games, and story lines. Her grown children still engage in "backseat" conversations—but now she's the one riding in back. This is her third book in a series for teens.

EDGE AfterWords

The Edge of Yesterday series is more than a book—it's a multimedia experience! Take it from me (Charley), there's a whole lot more to this adventure than what you read.

We've gone online to include YOU in the story at

edgeofyesterday.com

YOU CAN

- Get a sneak preview of my upcoming adventures
- Read interviews with some of my Heroes of History (like Albert Einstein)
- Find out how to learn like a Renaissance genius
- Pick up badges and stamps, as my adventure continues beyond Renaissance Florence to destinations in other centuries, to meet other Heroes of History (we may even travel to the future)
- Along the way, ask me anything about time travel . . . or just life in general. After all, I've experienced life as a teen in more than one place and time!

Expand your world. Explore other worlds. Share your dreams.
And share your journey with friends. Don't be trapped in one place in time—come join me today!

edgeofyesterday.com and **edgeofyesterdaybook.com**

CPSIA information can be obtained
at www.ICGtesting.com
Printed in the USA
FSHW010315211120
76041FS